The New Angels

Paula Milne

The New Angels

British Broadcasting Corporation

For Betty

Published by the
British Broadcasting Corporation
35 Marylebone High Street
London W1M 4AA

ISBN 0 563 17433 1

First published 1978

Printed in England by
Hollen Street Press Ltd
Slough, Berkshire

Contents

The Wrong Foot

Jean MacEwan regarded her face in the mirror, and decided, not for the first time, that she didn't think much of it. To most people it would have been considered a pretty face, but to its owner familiarity had, as Noel Coward said, bred contempt. Well, perhaps contempt is a little strong, Jean thought, putting her head on one side and squinting at her reflection in the grimy mirror. Perhaps boredom was nearer the mark. She wondered if other people got bored with their face. Hers distinctly irritated her. It was a deceitful face. Pretty, with round cheeks and delicate features, but still deceitful. It gave an impression of demureness; of placidity and contentment. In reality Jean knew herself to be none of these things.

Her nursing tutor back in Glasgow had once written of her in a progress report : 'Jean MacEwan, despite her somewhat fragile appearance, is an ambitious, highly efficient nurse. She has the natural authority born out of an innate sense of self-confidence. When she has proved she can temper this confidence with compassion, she will go far.'

And go far she did, though not necessarily in the way her nursing tutor imagined. After qualifying, she spent three years general nursing in various hospitals in her native Scotland, and then applied for the position of casualty Sister at St Angela's hospital. She had seen the application in one of the national nursing newspapers, and had answered it with little or no expectation of success. When she was granted an interview she still didn't allow her hopes to rise. At only twenty-five she was, after all, very young for such a post, and London casualty units were notoriously tough for even the most experienced Sisters. But she got the job. That is, she got the chance of a crack at it. She had been given a three months probationary contract.

So she had packed her bags, kissed her parents goodbye, and come down to London. She had arrived at Euston, grimy and exhausted on the Friday afternoon, and set about the irksome task of finding a flat, to find that there were none advertised either in the evening papers or on notice-boards. By six o'clock her patience, and her legs, gave up. She found the local YWCA hostel in the phone book and fixed herself up with a temporary room. The following morning she visited the hospital to collect her uniform. It was the first time she had returned to it since her interview, and she was once again struck by the grimness of the place. It loomed above her, large and intimidating, and she was assailed by doubt as to whether she really could be happy in such bleakly anonymous surroundings. She shrugged the doubt from her mind, telling herself it wasn't the building that was important anyway, it was the people inside it.

Jean's mouth suddenly felt dry. It was Monday morning and the start of her first day at St Angela's. She realised she was nervous, and was rather surprised. Nerves was not a condition she generally succumbed to, and she chided herself for indulging in it now. She *must* give the impression of confidence, even if she didn't feel it, for how else could she expect others to have confidence in her?

She pulled on her regulation mackintosh, and buttoned it up. After a final, cursory inspection of herself, she picked up her handbag and left the sanctuary of her room to face the day.

Jean's appointment was for nine o'clock, with one of the senior administrative nurses. After a brief, somewhat formal, welcome to St Angela's, she was directed to the casualty unit, where she was told the outgoing ward Sister, a Sister Clarke, would be waiting to start the handover.

The casualty unit looked a bit like a casualty itself. It consisted of a large, impersonal, open plan area, with various curtained-off cubicles on each side, and populated by several banks of chairs, where the patients sat while waiting for attention. The walls, Jean observed, as she entered and paused to look round, were covered in large, lurid posters. *Don't take your car for a drink!* one said bluntly, depicting a crashed car and an empty whisky bottle lying in the gutter beside it; *Smoking can damage your health!* announced another, showing an ashtray, brimming with charred cigarette ends. *Give Blood,* instructed yet another, showing a grateful patient being pumped with an inviting-looking pint of fresh blood. Jean's eyes roved round the unit, taking in the battered chairs, the graffiti-scarred walls and the floor tiles, shiny with wear. Student nurses and auxiliaries were weaving about self-importantly, sorting out blankets, stretchers and wheelchairs. On one of the chairs, oblivious of the bustle around him, sat a dishevelled, unwashed young man. His face was obscured by a mass of hair, and his body was partially obscured by a kind of make-shift harness, upon which hung all the apparatus of a one-man band. Tied round his head was a grimy, blood-stained handkerchief. He was playing a mouth organ, the sound of which echoed bleakly round the walls, and for no accountable reason, filled Jean with irritation.

At the far end of the unit, she could see a kind of glass cage, which she assumed to be the Sister's office. Squaring her shoulders slightly, she headed towards it.

The office was a testimony to organised chaos. Bits of paper and charts were taped to the glass walls. The desk was piled high with files and clipboards, mountains of paperwork cluttered every available surface. She went in.

A man, obviously a doctor, was in the office, talking into the telephone. 'I appreciate that,' he was saying wearily down the mouthpiece. 'But five days still constitutes a working week does it not? Even in pathology.' He paused, as the party at the other end started vigorously to defend themselves. 'I know you're overworked,' he interrupted at last, '*I'm* overworked. But I still manage, God knows how, but I *do* manage to get my job done.'

He glanced briefly at Jean while he waited for the answer.

'I haven't much choice but to wait, have I?' he went on irritably. 'In the meantime I'll send someone over for the first batch, so have them marked up and ready will you?' He hung up and started to scribble a note on a pad in front of him.

As Jean opened her mouth to introduce herself, the doctor cut her short. 'Right, Nurse – ' he had scarcely lifted his eyes from the pad – 'take this over to pathology will you? It's just down the corridor. I've some results need collecting. And on your way back, drop into X-ray, and see if a Mr Markham's plates are ready. I need them for a nine o'clock appointment.' Still without looking at her, he tore off a slip of paper and held it out to her. Jean stared at it silently.

'Quick as you can,' he said impatiently, waving the paper at her. 'There's a rush on.'

'I'm afraid there must be a mistake,' Jean said hesitantly, 'I've arranged to meet Sister Clarke here so she can . . .'

'Well Sister Clarke will just have to wait, won't she?' he replied bluntly, turning to look at her for the first time.

'Can't one of the junior nurses go . . . ?'

'They could,' he stared at her steadily, 'if I asked them, but I asked you. And I'm not in the habit of asking twice, Nurse.'

'Sister,' Jean corrected him, with some satisfaction. 'I take over from Sister Clarke at the end of the week. We start the handover today.'

He continued to regard her for a moment, then he rose, his manner abruptly changing gear, apparently all contrition for his earlier attitude. He put out his hand.

'Forgive me,' he said. 'I knew you were due in today, but it went clean out of my . . .' A trace of a smile played round his thin lips. 'Welcome to St Angela's, Sister . . . ?'

'MacEwan,' Jean replied, taking his hand.

'Doctor Sullivan. Casualty Registrar. We'll be working

together a good deal.' He perched on the desk, looking at her. 'From Scotland, right?'

'Glasgow.'

'Got yourself somewhere to live yet?'

'I've got a room in the YWCA for the time being,' Jean replied. 'Until I can get somewhere.'

'Why not try looking on one of the hospital notice-boards? People always seem to be advertising their flats on them.'

'I'll do that,' Jean said gratefully, suddenly warming to him. 'Thanks.'

Sullivan rose from the desk, and moved to the door. 'Well, now we've got the formalities out of the way, perhaps you'd like to pop round to pathology and get those specimens?' His voice was still pleasant, but his manner had somehow imperceptibly hardened. 'It's quite clearly signed, so you shouldn't have any problem.'

Jean stared at him in surprise. He shot her a swift, cold smile. 'And when Sister Clarke decides to grace us with her presence, I'll tell her you're here. All right?'

His hand, still holding the pathology slip, was pointedly held out towards her. Jean looked at it for a moment, and then back at his face. Slowly she reached out, took the slip of paper from his hand, and left the room.

Outside, she took a deep breath. A student nurse, bustling past her, mistook the look on her face for anger. But Jean was not so much angry, as rueful. As if she knew she had lost valuable ground, which would be difficult, if not impossible, to recover.

Student nurse Jay Harper watched Jean MacEwan leaving the casualty unit, and speculated as to whether this frail-looking creature could really be their new ward Sister. Next to her, David Preston, a student nurse in his third year, was preparing an instrument trolley. Jay closed the curtains separating them from the main casualty area, and

11

turned to help him.

'You wait,' David was saying, 'ten to one she'll be some starchy Scots spinster who'll have us all running round in circles, doing everything by the book.' He put an opthalmoscope on the trolley. 'I mean, why give the job to someone on the outside anyway? Plenty of people here would have jumped at it.'

'Sphyg . . .' Jay held out a hand, and he placed a blood pressure machine into it.

'She was probably quids in with the S.N.O.,' he continued, warming to his theme. 'The old pals act. They were probably at school together.' He smiled maliciously. 'Sharing girlish secrets behind the gymnasium.'

'What *are* you on about, Dave?'

'Our new Cas. Sister. Jean MacEwan or whatever she calls herself.'

'Make a habit of it do you?' Jay asked, rather more bluntly than she intended. 'Condemning people before you've even met them?'

'I don't like change, love. Particularly at management level. And when she starts fiddling around with the duty rotas, you won't be quite so keen either.'

'Who says she's going to do that?'

'She's the new broom isn't she?' David replied. 'And I don't have to spell it out about new brooms, do I?'

Jay turned to look at him. 'Let's face it, Dave,' she said, lowering her voice so that the patients waiting outside couldn't hear her, 'it isn't so much her being a new broom you object to, as the fact she's a woman.'

'Rubbish,' David managed to sound genuinely injured at the accusation.

'Is it?' Jay asked. 'Well, how come ever since Sister Clarke announced her retirement you've been going on about how it's the ideal job for a male nurse?'

'Because it is.'

'Meaning a woman can't do it just as well?'

He gave her one of his luxurious smiles. 'You said it.'

Jay put a stethoscope on the trolley and drew back the curtain. 'Well you're wrong,' she said, 'dead wrong.'

'We'll see, eh?' He was still smiling confidently.

'And you're wrong about something else,' Jay added, as she started to wheel out the trolley.

'Oh?'

'Jean MacEwan.' Jay nodded to where Jean was just re-entering the casualty unit. 'Starchy Scots spinster, isn't that what you called her?'

Unaware of David's eyes curiously assessing her, Jean made her way over to a woman in a Sister's uniform, whom she took to be Sister Clarke. She was talking to one of the junior nurses, and Jean waited until she'd finished before briefly introducing herself. Sister Clarke, a large, matronly woman in her late middle age, gave her a few perfunctory, but obviously genuine, words of greeting, and then launched into an enthusiastic run-down on the workings of the casualty unit. Judging by the reverent way she referred to doctors, and Doctor Sullivan in particular, Jean suspected she was the kind who accepted the hospital hierarchy without question. Sister Clarke continued to explain the way the unit operated, and Jean's eyes idly wandered over to the young busker, seated among the other patients. He was taking a furtive gulp from a beer bottle, which, when he became aware of her eyes on him, he quickly stashed away in a pocket under his harness of instruments.

'Do you get many of them?' Jean asked, interrupting Sister Clarke mid-flow.

'Many of what?'

Jean nodded towards the busker. 'His type. I wondered if you got a lot of them?'

Sister Clarke shot her a curious glance. 'Our share I suppose...'

'You're more tolerant than we were in Glasgow,' Jean replied. 'We showed them the door pretty sharp in the casualty unit up there.'

'They've the same right to medical care as anyone else, surely?' Sister Clarke asked, giving Jean a searching look.

'Assuming they're not just malingering,' Jean said. 'Or after a bed for the night.'

Sister Clarke gave her another sidelong glance, and then said simply : 'Well, that's for the doctor to decide isn't it?' She started to move towards the office. 'We'll run through the admission procedure, if you're ready?'

Inside the office, Sister Clarke gestured Jean to a chair while she sorted out some examples of admission cards.

'So, have you met him yet?' she asked, bringing a collection of cards to the desk, and sitting down next to Jean. Our Doctor Sullivan?'

'Briefly.'

Something in her tone made Sister Clarke glance over at her once again.

'He wasn't so much interested in getting acquainted,' Jean explained, 'as packing me off on an errand.' She looked through the glass wall of the office, into the casualty unit, where she could see Sullivan talking to a patient. 'I hope you don't have too many like him down here.'

'Like what?'

'Doctors who treat nurses like skivvies.'

'Is that what he did?'

'As good as.'

'He's not so bad really.' Sister Clarke started to lay the admission cards out on the desk in front of them. 'He's demanding of course, believes in giving respect where it's due . . . But when you've shown him you can do the job, he'll be fine.'

'Until then I'm guilty until proved innocent I suppose,' Jean asked, somewhat surprised at the sudden sourness in

14

her voice. 'I'm used to doctors treating nurses, particularly sisters, as equals, as part of the medical team. If he wants to play the "Great I Am", fine. So long as I don't have to listen to him!'

An awkward silence ensued. Sister Clarke was non-plussed. She had met nurses with progressive views before, but none who were prepared to air them quite so passionately. She decided to change the subject.

'Let's press on shall we?' she said. 'We've got a lot to get through, and I'm due at a Sister's meeting . . .' She picked up a stack of admission cards. 'Now then, the white cards we use for . . .'

At that moment the door opened, and Sullivan entered. 'Ah, Sister Clarke,' he said, his eyes flicking briefly over Jean, and then back to Sister Clarke. 'Get on to Bed State will you? See if Male Medical has a vacancy. I've a suspect cholecystitis I want to admit for observation.'

'Yes, Doctor.' Sister Clarke was already reaching for the telephone.

'And get Doctor Walker down here,' Sullivan added, as he turned to the door. 'There's a cartilage job in cubicle three I'd like a second opinion on.'

'Will do.' Sister Clarke started to dial an internal number.

Sullivan, about to withdraw, suddenly paused and glanced at Jean. 'Perhaps you'd like to help me out for a while, Sister . . . ?' He let the question hover.

'MacEwan,' Jean said flatly.

'After all,' Sullivan went on, smiling thinly, 'if you want to know what a job's all about, the best way is to get into the thick of it isn't it? And you certainly won't learn much tucked away in here, will you?' Without waiting for a reply, he strode out.

Jean took a deep breath, counted to ten, and glanced over at Sister Clarke. But she was talking on the telephone and appeared not to have heard the interchange. Jean, with ill-concealed bad grace, scraped back her chair and left the room. It was only then, as she replaced the telephone on to the receiver, that Sister Clarke acknowledged that she had in fact registered Sullivan's words, and Jean's response to them. She allowed herself a small smile of wry amusement.

Jean spent the rest of the morning in a whirl of activity, ferrying patients through to Sullivan for examination, familiarising herself with all the nurses working under her, and trying to fathom the complex admission procedure paper-work. Some two hours later, while grabbing a snatched lunch of sandwiches and coffee at her desk, she glanced through the glass walls of the office to see that the young busker was still sitting awaiting attention. Having finished off one bottle of beer, he was making a start on his second. As he gulped at it, he became aware of a pair of eyes observing him. He lowered the bottle and saw a middle-aged woman, wearing a flowered hat and matching suit, stonily regarding him from her seat a few yards away. The busker solemnly raised his bottle to her, in a mock toast.

'To all those poor souls less fortunate than ourselves,' he said. 'Your health, madam.' Keeping his eyes defiantly on her face, he put the bottle to his lips and drank. Embarrassed, the woman hastily averted her eyes, and the busker smiled, as if he were the victor in some unspoken battle.

Jean, watching from the office, frowned. The woman's discomfort was obvious and she was annoyed with the busker for causing it. She went out into the unit, where David Preston passed her, wheeling a patient. She called out to him.

'Mr Preston, isn't it?'

David paused and turned back. Jean lowered her voice fractionally. 'Has the doctor seen him yet?' she asked, nodding towards the busker.

David followed her gaze and shook his head. 'Not that I know of . . . '

'Why not?' Jean replied. 'The sooner the better, I'd say.'

'No good asking me,' David said, and then pointed to Sullivan, who was just entering the office behind them. 'He's the guv'nor, ask him.'

Sullivan was on the phone when Jean re-entered the office.

'You *are* the woman's GP, mate,' he was saying down the mouthpiece, glancing up briefly as Jean entered. 'Who said anything about working miracles? I'm just asking you to refer patients early enough, so that we've got a fair chance of doing something for them – ' he strummed his fingers impatiently – 'if you'd sent her along to us when she first complained of her headaches we might have had a chance to do something for her. As it is . . .' He paused, finally allowing the other man to get a word in edgeways. But not for long. 'You bet I'm going to make it an official complaint,' he cut in, and abruptly hung up, crashing the telephone on to the receiver with such force that the whole desk shook.

'Problems?' Jean enquired politely.

'GPS.' Sullivan retorted, as if that explained everything. 'Spend half their time on their backsides, dishing out tran-quillisers, and call it a day's work.'

'If you've got a moment,' said Jean cautiously, 'we've got another problem.'

'They want to try working in here once in a while,' Sullivan continued. 'See how they like it.' He broke off and looked at her. 'What kind of problem?'

'Can't you hear it?' Jean crossed to the door, and opened it, so that the sound of the busker's mouth organ flooded into the office. Sullivan stared at her blankly.

'There's obviously not much wrong with him, is there?' Jean said. 'So I was hoping you could squeeze him in now. The quicker you examine him, the quicker we'll be shot of him. And then perhaps we can have some peace.'

Sullivan said nothing, his pale eyes impassively resting on

her. Jean, slightly disconcerted by his scrutiny, closed the door and leant against it.

'He's disturbing the other patients,' she said pointedly, as if some further explanation was necessary.

'You've had complaints have you?'

'No, but . . .'

'Perhaps it isn't the other patients he's disturbing,' Sullivan said, 'as much as you.'

Jean felt a flood of angry colour coming into her cheeks.

'I don't know what kind of cosy cottage hospital set-up you're used to, love,' Sullivan went on, before she could collect herself sufficiently to speak. 'But you're going to have to get used to his type here, and worse. A lot worse.' He started for the door.

'So you won't see him?'

Sullivan paused and turned back. 'I'll see him, all right, Sister,' he said. 'But since, as you say, there's obviously not much wrong with him, he's going to have to wait his turn isn't he? I don't know about you, but urgent cases come first in my book,' and he left the room, banging the door closed behind him.

Jean bit her lip. She felt angry and humiliated. Angry because of Sullivan's unreasonable attitude, and humiliated because she had allowed herself to respond emotionally to it. The whole day had been a disaster from the moment she encountered him. Why was she acting like this? Why did she let that busker annoy her, and make herself look so stupid and bigoted in front of a man like Sullivan? He obviously thought nurses were dumb anyway, and her performance was only going to endorse his opinion. She would have to prove him wrong, it was that simple. She would have to make him see that she was perfectly capable of making an independent decision. Then perhaps he would stop barking at her like a sergeant major, and start treating her as an equal. Even as the thought passed through her mind, another one followed it. She smiled to herself and squared her shoulders. With a renewed sense of purpose, she left the room.

Outside, she saw David Preston, talking to an ambulance driver. She beckoned to him, and he crossed over to her.

'Directly a cubicle falls free, I want you to put Larry Adler there in it,' she said, indicating the busker. 'And get his wound ready for me to examine will you?'

David hesitated. 'The doctor's still tied up with that haemorrhage case . . .'

'No need to worry the doctor,' Jean said. 'I'm going to see to him myself.' She started to move away, when David stopped her.

'Doctor Sullivan usually likes to deal with the patients himself,' he began. 'It's a kind of house rule with him . . .'

'Is it?' Jean replied coolly. 'Well I'm going to have to bend the rules for once aren't I?' She smiled, seeing David's expression. 'I'll take full responsibility, Mr Preston. If that's what's worrying you.'

David looked at her retreating back. 'You bet your sweet life you will, darlin',' he muttered, and then ambled back to resume his conversation with the ambulance driver.

'You did what?'

'I discharged him,' Jean replied. It was an hour later and she was facing a taut-faced Sullivan across Sister Clarke's desk.

'On whose authority?'

'Look . . .' Jean said patiently. 'It was a straightforward cut. It didn't even need saturing. I sent him to X-ray, but they found nothing, so I cleaned it up and sent him on his way. I'm quite prepared to take responsibility for it.'

'Wrong, love,' Sullivan snapped. 'I'm the registrar, and if anything happens to that patient, *I'll* be the one held responsible.'

'Nothing's *going* to happen to him.'

'Since I was deprived of seeing him myself, I can't be sure of that, can I?'

'You're just going to have to trust my judgement then, aren't you?'

'And what happens if we get someone in complaining of a chest pain?' Sullivan demanded. 'Will you take it upon yourself to discharge them too? Maybe send a suspect coronary packing with a few indigestion tablets, because you fancy some more of your amateur diagnosis?'

'I *am* a qualified nurse you know . . .'

'. . . And *I* am the senior doctor on duty, and as such it's my duty to see *all* the patients, not just a chosen few weeded out by you.'

Jean stared at him angrily. 'I was trying to reduce your work load.'

'My work load, Sister, is my problem.'

'Not when it affects my nurses it's not,' Jean retorted. 'If you insist on seeing every patient,' she went on, feeling that at last she was on solid ground, 'no matter how trivial their condition, it's no wonder we're as behind as we are. Half those patients have been waiting out there since nine this morning . . . And I suppose you expect my nurses to stay late until you've seen every last one of them?'

'I doubt that'll be necessary.'

'But if it was,' Jean said, determined to press the point, 'you would?'

'Yes,' he replied unflinchingly, 'I would.'

'That's hardly fair on them, is it?'

'I'm not so much concerned with being fair to your nurses, Sister, as being fair to the patients.'

'By keeping them hanging round half the day?'

'By ensuring they get the best possible medical attention. Which means being seen by an experienced, qualified doctor, who knows what he's doing.'

Jean stared at him, almost too angry to speak.

'I repeat,' she said at last, 'I am perfectly capable of dressing a simple head wound.'

'I'm sure you are,' Sullivan said. 'So in future I'll thank you to stick to doing just that. And leave the diagnosis to those trained for the job.' He turned to go, suggesting that as far as he was concerned, the conversation was over.

'I thought part of your job was to delegate?' Jean demanded. 'Well, isn't it? Isn't that what being head of a team means? To encourage mutual trust? There seems to be precious little of it round here.'

Sullivan paused, and turned back. 'I delegate, Sister,' he said harshly, 'if and when someone's proved they can do the job.'

'And how are they ever going to do that if you won't give them the chance?' Jean retorted.

He fell silent, his pale eyes travelling impassively over her face. 'I don't think you're worried about your nurses, or delegating or anything else,' he said. 'I think you're worried because a noisy young drunk was cluttering up your nice new casualty unit, and creating a bad impression for you. So you want shot of him. Out of sight, out of mind.'

'Nonsense!'

'You didn't think to discharge any of the others did you?' he pointed out. 'That boy with the cut hand, or the old girl with the sprained ankle. If it really was my work load you were worried about, how come they didn't get their marching orders as well?'

Jean opened her mouth to reply, when another, vaguely familiar voice cut in.

'Doctor Sullivan?'

They swung round to face the door, where Miss Lewis, the Senior Nursing Officer, was staring at them coldly. She addressed herself initially to Sullivan.

'If you have a complaint to make about one of my

21

Sisters, Doctor Sullivan, may I suggest you go through official channels? Rather than indulging in a slanging match where everyone can hear you.'

Sullivan glanced at Jean, and then back at Miss Lewis. 'I might just do that thing,' he said, and pushed his way past her, through the door.

Miss Lewis turned to Jean. 'Sister MacEwan, isn't it?'

Jean nodded.

'I just came to welcome you in. Not a very auspicious start, is it?'

'He's not the easiest person to get along with, you know,' Jean replied defensively.

'Sister Clarke seemed to manage without too much trouble.'

'Yes, well, Sister Clarke . . .' Jean began, then paused. She glanced at Miss Lewis and thought better of what she was about to say. 'She and I seem to look at things rather differently,' she ended up, somewhat lamely.

' "Things" in this case being the job?'

'Aspects of it, anyway.'

'And more specifically Doctor Sullivan?'

Sensing a trap, Jean made no reply.

'If you're having difficulties in your working relationship, Sister, and judging by what I just heard, you are, it's better to get it out into the open now isn't it? Before any more damage is done.'

Jean frowned. 'Damage?'

'It's hardly the best example to set your junior nurses is it?'

'I don't know that it's much worse than bowing and scraping to someone simply because they happen to be both male and a doctor,' Jean said heatedly. She shot Miss Lewis a quick look, afraid she might have gone too far. 'I'm sorry,' she added, 'but that seems to be the treatment he's used to.'

'Or the way you want to see it,' Miss Lewis said.

'Since this is your first day, I'm surprised you've had time to see what kind of treatment he gets. Let alone jump to conclusions about it.'

'It's certainly the impression I got.'

'And what about the impression you're giving? Or don't you consider that important?' Miss Lewis glanced at the open door behind her, and moved to close it. 'Within hours of setting foot in the place, you've managed not only to alienate one of your colleagues, but to do it in such a place and manner so as to adversely affect the students working under you. Students to whom you are responsible, Sister, and who look to you to set an example.' Jean was about to reply, but Miss Lewis rattled on, unabated. 'And don't fool yourself they're not aware of it. Friction like this very quickly percolates down, and before you know it, sides are being taken and the entire working team is affected.' She drew a breath, and looked Jean squarely in the face. 'Well, fortunately for you, not everyone attaches the same importance to first impressions. Otherwise I might well not have let this matter rest here, believe me.' She placed a hand on the door knob, and paused. 'There are times,' she said, almost as an afterthought, 'when we all resent the status of doctors, Sister. But the real trick is not to give them the satisfaction of knowing it. It's called tactics,' and she left the room, leaving Jean with her unspoken words of protest still on her lips.

Jay Harper pulled the cubicle curtain closed and turned to confront David, who was struggling into his overcoat.

'Well could *you* have stood up to Sullivan the way she did?'

'No . . .' David smiled languidly. 'But then I wouldn't have got myself into that situation in the first place.'

'In other words, you'd have played safe, stuck to the rules and done as the doctor ordered?' Jay paused, and then went

23

on more reasonably. 'Don't you ever get sick of it, Dave? Dancing in attendance to them? "Yes, Doctor, no Doctor, anything you say, Doctor". Well, don't you?'

David sighed. 'Look, if we all started doing as she did, by-passing the doctors, questioning them, where would it end? Hospitals are run on discipline, break that down and there'd be chaos.'

'Sounds like a handy excuse to me,' Jay said sullenly. 'For not defending ourselves.'

'You've had your chance, Jay,' David said irritably. 'Hundreds of them. I've not heard you doing much about it. And you know why? Because you know damned well it would end up like today's little effort. With you being hauled up in front of the S.N.O. with a complaint hanging over you.'

Jay stared at him. 'D'you really think he'll complain?'

David shrugged. 'You know Sullivan. He's not exactly the type to make idle threats, is he?'

Sister Clarke shot a surreptitious glance at Jean, sitting at the desk. Her face was cupped disconsolately in her hand, and she was absently doodling on the blotter. Sister Clarke reached for her coat, on a hanger behind the door.

'Anyone can get off on the wrong foot can't they?' she said, suddenly feeling sorry for Jean. She looked very young and vulnerable, hunched over the desk.

'And it couldn't have been easy,' she went on. 'That kind of confrontation never is.' She paused and then added, 'If it was, I might have done it myself by now.'

Jean glanced at her in surprise.

'Don't think I haven't wanted to,' Sister Clarke said, pulling on her coat. 'And I've had the opportunity, countless opportunities. When he marches in here the way he does, issuing his instructions, I've often felt like . . .' she broke off . . . 'But when it comes to it I'm just not that sort of person. I never was. I can never find the right words. Or the guts, depending on how you look at it.'

Jean sighed. 'I'm beginning to think it takes more guts to keep quiet.'

'That depends on how you look at it as well, doesn't it?' Sister Clarke replied. 'All the same — ' her tone was almost wistful – it would have been nice to have done it, just *once* before I left. To prove to myself that I could, if nothing else.' She glanced at Jean, slightly embarrassed, and quickly changed the subject. 'I've got my car today. Can I drop you anywhere?'

Jean stood up and reached for her coat. 'It's OK, the bus stop's only round the corner, and I want to go to the shops on my way.' She pulled her coat on, and then shot Sister Clarke an anxious look. 'D'you really think he meant it? Doctor Sullivan? About making a complaint about me?'

'I'm afraid he did. When Doctor Sullivan says he's going to make a complaint about someone, he invariably does it.' She suddenly smiled. 'At least twice at week.'

Jean smiled in relief, and together they headed for the door. As they reached it, Sullivan entered. He glanced briefly at Jean, and then turned to Sister Clarke, holding out a folder of patient's notes towards her. 'Put this somewhere where it won't get lost, Sister. I'll need it first thing in the morning.'

Sister Clarke however, instead of taking the folder, glanced at Jean, and then back at him.

'Perhaps you could see to it yourself this once, Doctor Sullivan,' she said. 'We're just on our way home,' and before he could reply, she left the office. Jean, following her, caught a glimpse of Sullivan's startled face, before she shut the door. She turned to Sister Clarke with a grin.

'Well,' she said, some of her former spirit returning, 'I think you might have just taught him a lesson there.'

Sister Clarke gave her a small smile, and pulled on her

gloves. 'I think perhaps we've all learnt something today, don't you, dear?' And without waiting for an answer, she waddled off up the corridor.

Decisions

It hadn't occurred to Anna to take up nursing until some three weeks after her father's death. In the meantime she had applied for countless clerical posts, only to discover that either the salary was too low, or the type of work too monotonous. Then one Friday evening, while waiting at the bus stop after an unsuccessful interview, she saw Sarah Lloyd Smith again.

She was walking down the road with another nurse, both in uniform, they were laughing as they walked, their heads close together as if sharing a private joke. Anna had a sudden, inexplicable urge to speak to Sarah, but the bus came and the moment was lost.

Afterwards, Anna found herself thinking about Sarah, or more specifically, about the night she had spent at the hospital, and the events that had led up to it.

It had all started on the day of that dreadful row, a week after her return to her parents' home in Croydon. She remembered she had dreamt she was back with Keith. The dream was so vivid that when she woke, it took her several seconds to realise where she was. For a moment her head swam with persistent images of her dream, of Keith's face lying on the pillow next to her own. But as she blinked away the last remnants of sleep, she saw the pillow beside her was empty, and she was relieved. The dream, acute in its detail, disturbed her, and for once she found she was grateful for reality.

She raised herself up and looked at the room. It was the room she had lived in as a child, and it still bore the traces of that childhood. A framed swimming certificate hung above the bed, and on another wall, a faded montage of pin-ups, depicting past pop idols. She sank against the pillows, savouring the warmth of the bed. She wanted the last shreds of the dream to leave her before she got up to face the day. Downstairs she could hear the faint clatter of breakfast dishes and the familiar murmur of her parents' voices.

Lying there she could almost imagine she was a child again, and the thought was somehow comforting, arousing memories of other mornings in this same bed, when the prospect of a new day was something to anticipate eagerly instead of dread. And dread it she did. She dreaded the reproachful silence from her father, and her mother's over anxious attempts to cover it with trivial conversation.

Abruptly she got up, pulled on a dressing-gown, and crossed to the window. In the back garden she could see Emma, her small daughter, playing in a make-shift sand pit, and the sight filled her with new strength. There must be no going back, she told herself, if not for your sake, for Emma's, and keeping that thought resolutely in mind, she left the room and went downstairs.

Howard was in the kitchen, polishing off the remains of a fried egg. Anna dutifully kissed his proffered cheek, before sitting down opposite him.

'Where's Mother?'

'In the garden. She went to play with Emma.' He didn't bother to lift his eyes from his plate. Anna poured herself a cup of coffee, and picked up the morning paper. As she folded it, she glanced at her father's impassive face. He was a tall, solidly built man in his late middle age. Like his daughter, there was something of the decision maker about him. But his decisiveness was born out of a kind of tenacious refusal to acknowledge that the world was changing around him. He was dressed for work, in a dark suit and tie. Having finished his egg, he pushed it to one side, and rose from the table. He moved to the dresser, and started rummaging through one of the drawers.

'What are you looking for?' Anna asked.

'Aspirin,' he replied shortly, 'I've a headache.'

Wordlessly Anna got up and located the aspirin bottle. She filled a glass with water, and passed it, together with the pills, to Howard. He gulped back the aspirin, returned the glass, and left the room. Anna breathed a small sigh of relief, as if she had been reprieved. But no sooner had the thought crossed her mind, than he re-appeared in the doorway, struggling into his top coat.

'Well, have you thought over what I said? About getting a job?'

'Yes, Daddy, I'm going to start looking today.'

'And you really think you're going to get one do you? Just like that?'

'Why not?'

'You've no skill have you?' he said impatiently. 'You can't even type.'

'So I'll learn a skill.' Anna shrugged, crossing back to the table and sitting down. 'I'm not completely helpless.' She picked up the paper, as if hoping it would somehow deter him, but it only seemed to aggravate his mood. He moved over and plucked the newspaper out of her hands.

'At least look at me when I'm talking to you.'

'Daddy,' Anna carefully monitored her voice so that any anger she might feel was not immediately apparent, 'I *will* get a job. I know it won't be easy, but I'll get one. If that's what's worrying you, forget it. Because the problem's as good as solved.'

'That child out there is what worries me, Anna,' Howard said, pointing towards the window, and the little girl beyond it. 'Her future is what worries me, which you seem to be giving precious little thought to.'

'I've thought of nothing else,' Anna replied dully.

'Strange way you have of showing it.'

'And staying with Keith,' Anna said, finally allowing the anger to well up and spill over, 'staying married to a man I no longer care for, that's good for her future is it?'

He made no answer.

'Well, is it?'

'It's a damn sight better than uprooting her from her

home and father, and everything she . . .'

'Anyone would think it was easy,' Anna interrupted, 'walking out that door, leaving everything and everyone I've known for the last four years . . . Well, the easy way, Daddy, would have been to stay put. To grin and bear it, and say nothing.'

'The easy way, Anna,' Howard responded promptly, 'is to do precisely what you're doing. To run away. To duck your responsibility. That *is* what you're doing, isn't it?'

'You tell me,' Anna replied, aware that her answer was both evasive and petulant. 'You're obviously the big expert on responsibility around here.'

He regarded her for a moment, and then picked up his briefcase from a chair, and started for the door.

'Daddy?' Anna half rose from the table. Suddenly she didn't want them to end their conversation there. She wanted all the doubts and tensions out in the open. But Howard didn't seem to hear, and continued to the door.

'We've never once finished a conversation,' Anna called after him. 'Can't we just finish this one? We'll have to eventually, won't we?'

For a moment it seemed that Howard was going to ignore her, then he paused and turned back. 'A conversation,' he said at last, 'implies a duologue. Give and take. Listening to another's point of view . . .'

'I do listen to your point of view!'

'No, you don't,' Howard said. 'You've never listened to anyone's point of view, Anna, except your own. That's the problem.'

A second later, Anna heard the front door swing shut behind him, and the sound filled her with desolation. She crossed to the window, and looked absently out at her daughter and mother, playing happily together by the sand pit. Except she wasn't looking so much at them, as at the garden and nearby houses surrounding them, as if the answer to some unspoken question lay out there, just out of reach.

Meanwhile, a few miles away, in St Angela's hospital, another girl was apprehensively looking through a window. The girl was Sarah Lloyd Smith, and the window was a small porthole in the doors that led into the intensive care unit.

Although Sarah stoically tried to convince herself that this ward was like any other she had worked on, she couldn't help feeling intimidated by the complex looking machinery and unconscious patients lying helplessly on their beds. The reputation of the ward preceded it. It was known to be one of the toughest and most arduous to work in, not only because the patients were so critically ill, but because their dependence on the medical team was total, and consequently any error of judgement could be fatal. Many nurses welcomed such responsibility, but to Sarah it was an awesome prospect. The ratio of death in such a ward was inevitably higher than most, and the idea of it dismayed her. Until now she had managed, with a surprising degree of success, to avoid such traumas, and as a result she felt ill-equipped to deal with them. She dithered hesitantly by the doors for another moment, and then, bolstering herself with the thought she was only due to work on the ward for a few days at the most, she pushed open the doors, and entered.

Once inside, she was promptly approached by another nurse, in her third year. Sarah recognised her type immediately. Ebullient, resilient and positively bristling with zealous energy. A born survivor, and a born nurse. Her name tag, pinned on to her uniform collar, said 'Katey Betts, student nurse.'

Katey briefly introduced herself, discovered that Sarah had been sent by the nursing officer to help them out during a temporary staff shortage, and then took her over to the

Sister on duty. The Sister, a harassed, gaunt-faced girl in her late twenties, looked at Sarah in dismay.

'A second year? But I asked for a *third* year . . .'

'They're going to try and send one along later to replace me,' Sarah replied.

'They'd better,' the Sister said bluntly, 'or I'll have to get on to the agency again.' She put her head on one side, and shot Sarah a shrewd look. 'Have you ever worked in intensive care before?'

Sarah shook her head.

'Well have you ever been inside the unit before?' asked the Sister, with mounting irritation.

'Once,' Sarah replied. 'The nursing tutor showed us around. And my father's told me about it of course . . .'

'Your father?'

'He's the consultant surgeon here . . .' As she said it, Sarah was aware of how absurdly trite it sounded. The Sister and Katey clearly shared her view, as they exchanged meaningful looks.

'All right, Nurse Betts,' the Sister said to Katey in a resigned tone. 'You know the drill.'

'This way.' Katey touched Sarah's arm, and led the way into the centre of the ward.

'Where are we going?'

'In a minute I'll give you the guided tour,' Katey replied. 'Show you what we do. But first off, you can show us what *you* can do, OK?'

'OK,' Sarah answered, with considerably more confidence than she felt, and then found herself adding. 'As long as it's nothing too complicated . . .'

Katey smiled. 'Going to need all your powers of concentration this, love. Definitely.' She paused in front of a vacant, unmade bed. 'You worked with Sister Young yet, on female medical?'

'Yes . . .'

'You'll have heard her sermon on beds then.' Katey went on. 'A made bed is a happy bed, all that?'

'Yes . . .'

Katey pointed to the bed in front of them. 'Put that one out of its misery then will you? While I go for coffee,' and dumping a pile of clean linen into Sarah's hands, she walked out of the ward.

'Hold still, darling, come on.'

Emma screwed her eyes into small slits, as Anna wiped her protesting mouth with a piece of kitchen paper. At the sink, Joan watched them as she washed up the breakfast dishes.

'You really shouldn't keep plying her with chocolate, Mother,' Anna said, as she released the little girl, who immediately headed back into the garden.

'Well,' Joan shrugged, 'you're only young once.'

Such a reply was typical of her mother, Anna reflected. A cliché for every occasion. She immediately felt a twinge of disloyalty at the thought, and looked for some way to atone for it.

'I'll do the dishes, if there's something else you want to get on with . . . ?'

Joan declined the offer with a small shake of the head. 'You'd better get dressed, if you're still going job hunting.'

'I thought I'd look at the ads. first,' Anna replied, picking up the newspaper. 'See if there's anything worth following up.'

A moment of silence followed, broken by Joan, turning to face her daughter. Her tone was cautious. 'I hope all this is going to be worth it, Anna.'

'Worth what?' Anna knew perfectly well what was coming, but she felt impelled to let her mother pursue the point. Perhaps if there was some way of making her mother understand, there was a chance her father might. But even as she thought it, she knew it was hopeless. People only extend understanding when they want to, and Howard had made his feelings quite clear on that score.

'All this trouble,' Joan went on. 'Making your father miserable. Not to mention what poor Keith must be feeling.'

'You've left someone out, haven't you?' Anna asked mildly. 'Aren't I making *you* miserable as well?'

Joan glanced at her sharply. 'It goes without saying.'

'And you never do say anything, do you, Mother?' Anna said gently. 'Much less complain.'

'What's the good in that?' Joan replied. 'Complaining never got anyone anywhere.'

'Yes, well unfortunately I don't seem to be made of such stern stuff.' To her surprise, Anna sounded genuinely rucful. 'I'm a born complainer, me.'

'Nonsense!'

Anna stood up and carried her empty coffee cup over to the sink. Through the kitchen window they could see Emma, still playing in the garden.

'I know how senseless all this must seem to you, Mother,' she said after a moment. 'And selfish. But I'm beginning to think you have to be selfish sometimes . . . Or else you end up simply living to please other people, fulfilling their expectations but never your own.'

Joan abruptly pulled the plug from the sink. 'That's all very well, Anna,' she said. 'But you've a child now, remember?'

'So?'

'So you've got someone else besides yourself to consider, haven't you?'

'It always comes back to that, doesn't it?" Anna said wearily.

'It's the truth.'

'And you really think she'll thank me for it, do you? When she's grown up? That she'll thank me for wasting my life in a loveless marriage?'

'Don't be melodramatic.'

'Of course she won't,' Anna went on, ignoring her mother's remark. 'Any more than I'd thank you, if I thought that's what you'd done.'

Joan said nothing. Unintentionally Anna had stumbled on a home truth, and she was temporarily disconcerted. She squeezed out a cloth and started to mop down the table.

'Supposing you do manage to get a job?' she said eventually, aware she was changing the subject. 'Who's going to look after Emma?'

'I'll have to find a crèche,' Anna replied.

'It won't be easy.'

'I know, but what's the alternative?'

'I suppose – ' Joan hesitated – 'I could take her.' She looked doubtfully at Anna. 'If you really are determined about this, I could have her while you were at work, during the day. At least to start with, until you've found your feet.'

Anna stared at her mother in surprise. 'Would you really?'

'Why not? Provided your father agreed . . .'

Anna returned to the table and sat down. 'There's not much chance of that, is there?' she said flatly. 'Not the way he feels at the moment.'

'Why not ask him?'

'What's the point? We both know what he'd say.'

'You don't know until you try, do you?' Joan said a trifle impatiently. 'Why not meet him for lunch somewhere? Try and talk him round?'

'Neutral ground?' Anna asked dryly.

Joan moved to sit opposite her daughter. 'If you'd just talk to him, Anna . . . make him feel you need his help again. That's why it's all gone wrong between you. Because you've done something as important as this, without even talking to him. If he still felt you needed him, needed his advice,

I'm sure he'd come round. In fact I know he would.'

'A bit like play acting isn't it?'

'Sometimes it's necessary to play act,' Joan said, brusquely rising from the table and moving back to the sink. 'If it helps save other people's feelings.'

'Is that what you do with him, Mother?'

Joan bit her lip. Anna, like her father, had a disturbing way of seizing on the truth which unsettled her. Although why the truth should unsettle her so much, was a question she preferred not to ask.

'We're not talking about me,' she said at last. 'We're talking about you, Anna. If you want your father's help over this, the only way you're going to get it, is to ask for it.'

'And if he decides not to give it?'

'That's just a chance you'll have to take, isn't it?' Joan untied her apron and hung it on the back of the kitchen door. 'But someone has to bend a bit, make the first move . . .' She paused, and then added : 'Believe me, you could grow old waiting for him to do it.'

After she'd gone, Anna sat deliberating for some minutes. She realised it wasn't Howard's help she wanted, as much as his approval for her actions, and the discovery troubled her. His approval was something she should have outgrown, but she hadn't. She needed it as much as when she was a child, when winning his approval was synonymous with winning his affection. The thought filled her with resentment. Not simply for herself, but for her mother. Over the years Howard had dominated them into acquiescence, because it was easier to give in than to challenge his authority. And here she was about to do it again. Well, even if it *was* his approval she was after, she told herself, she also needed his help. And it was better, or so she argued, to make a minor compromise with her father than to return to her empty life with Keith. Anything was better than that.

She went to the telephone and dialled Howard's office.

His secretary answered the phone, and recognising Anna's voice, promptly connected her with Howard. He sounded gruff, and surprised to hear from her.

"I thought perhaps we could meet for lunch somewhere?' Anna said. 'To talk things over.'

'If you think it'll help,' he replied. They arranged to meet in an Italian restaurant near his office. Just as Anna was about to ring off, he added : 'And bring those aspirin will you? I can't seem to shift this headache.'

Anna replaced the receiver and collected the aspirin from the kitchen table. In case she should forget later, she put the bottle in her handbag. She was about to go upstairs to dress, when her mother entered.

'I thought I heard you talking to someone,' she said, glancing round the room.

'You did,' Anna replied. 'I rang Daddy. We're meeting for lunch.'

Joan smiled. 'Good girl,' she said, her relief obvious. 'That wasn't so difficult was it?'

Anna smiled non-committally, and said nothing. As she climbed the stairs to her room, she comforted herself with the thought that if she hadn't won Howard's approval for the phone call, she had clearly won Joan's.

.

It occurred to Sarah that if ever Katey Betts chucked in nursing, she could become a first-class tourist guide. She had a way of rattling off diverse snatches of information that could only be described as unnerving. One by one she went through the patients in the intensive care unit, describing their conditions, prognosis and treatment. It was only when she paused for breath that Sarah was able to get a question in.

'What's the matter with him?' she asked, indicating a youth with a battered face, covered in a fine mesh of wires and dressings.

'Multiple injuries and possible kidney damage,' Katey replied. 'Some gang set on him at a football match. We're still waiting for him to regain consciousness.' She moved to the next bed, the empty one that Sarah had recently made up.

'And here we had a barbiturate overdose, but we lost her just before you came on duty.' Her tone, momentarily, became reflective. 'Something you have to get used to in here. The patients are usually unconscious, and you'd think, if you do lose them, that it wouldn't hit you so hard, wouldn't you? Because they've been out for the count most of the time anyway . . .' She paused, and then went on : 'Except being like that, it makes them that much more dependent on you. So if you do lose them, you end up feeling worse somehow. Like you're to blame.' She glanced at Sarah and roused herself. 'Still, as I said. That's something you have to get used to.' She grinned. 'Either that or go mad.' She started to bustle towards the door. 'Come on, I'll show you the waiting area.'

The waiting area consisted of a large, anonymous room, lined with chairs and with a bed in one corner. A middle-aged man, wearing the uniform of a London Transport bus driver, was sitting in one of the chairs, smoking a cigarette. He looked dishevelled with tiredness and anxiety. As Katey entered he stood up expectantly.

'You still here, Mr Wyatt?' Katey asked. 'You'll take root soon.'

'I prefer to stay, Nurse,' he replied mildly. 'Just in case . . . There's no . . . ?'

Katey shook her head. 'He's still unconscious. We'll tell you as soon as there's any change.' She looked at him carefully. 'You want to sit with him a bit more?'

'If I'm not in anyone's way . . .'

'Clear it with the Sister as you go in,' Katey replied, smiling. 'Or else she'll think I'm taking liberties.'

'Right,' as he spoke Mr Wyatt was heading towards the door. 'Thanks, Nurse.'

Katey waited for the door to close behind him. 'The father of the kid hurt at the football match,' she explained briefly, and then added. 'That's something else you have to get used to. The relatives. Sometimes they need more nursing than the patients.'

'What happens . . .' Sarah began cautiously . . . 'if you lose a patient, like that overdose girl. Who tells them?'

'The relatives?' Katey thought a moment. 'The doctor usually. Or Sister. But if they're busy or – ' she shot Sarah a curious look – 'why, does the idea bother you?'

'I've never had to do it before,' Sarah confessed. 'I'm not sure I could.'

'You will,' Katey said in her matter-of-fact way. 'It's like I keep saying, love. You can get used to anything in time. Even that.' And she bustled out, leaving Sarah looking bleakly round the empty room.

It was one of those cheap and cheerful Italian restaurants, packed to the hilt with lunch-time eaters. Waiters, with perilous loads of pasta and carafes of red wine, weaved their way in and out of the tables.

Anna was watching a group of teenage girls at a nearby table. It was someone's birthday, and they were clearly out to have a good time if it killed them. At the sound of their raucous, high-pitched giggles, Howard's hand fluttered up to his brow in a familiar gesture of irritation.

'How's the headache?' Anna asked.

'Dreadful. And it's likely to remain that way with that din going on. Like trying to eat in a school playground.' He cast his eyes around the jostling eaters, looking for a waiter.

'Don't make a fuss, Dad, please,' Anna implored. 'They don't mean any harm.'

'It's the old story.' He lowered his eyes to his half-finished lasagne. 'Lack of consideration.'

They continued eating for a moment in silence, then Howard said: 'So, have you decided what you're going to do?'

'Do?'

'I assumed you'd come to some kind of decision. Hence the sudden lunch invitation . . .'

Anna hesitated a moment before replying. 'I told you my decision this morning, Daddy. Anyway,' she added, 'it was Mother's idea we should meet for lunch.'

'Oh?'

'She seemed to think it might clear the air.'

Howard said nothing, and toyed with his food a moment. Then he looked up at her. 'Exactly what is it you want from me, Anna?' he asked. 'My approval? You want me to condone your actions, is that it?'

'Not necessarily . . .'

'Because if so,' he went on, 'I can't oblige I'm afraid. And nothing you've said to date is likely to make me change that view.' He paused. 'You had a good marriage . . . You might not appreciate it at this moment, or want to appreciate it, but you did. Keith's a good man. You're not likely to find another like him.'

'I don't want to find another like him,' Anna replied wearily. 'I don't want another man, full stop. Not at the moment anyway.'

'What *do* you want then?'

She put down her fork and looked at him. 'I got married when I was nineteen, Daddy. Nineteen! When other girls were going to university, starting their careers, going abroad, I was choosing fitted carpets and three piece suites.'

'Whose fault's that?'

'All right, it was mine. I know you didn't want me to marry him, I know you thought we were too young. And I

41

should have listened to you, I admit it. But what am I supposed to do, pay for that mistake for the rest of my life?'

'As I remember at the time,' Howard said, 'you said you were going into it with your eyes "wide open" . . .'

'And if you remember, *you* said I was going into it wearing the "romantic blinkers of a nineteen-year-old".' Anna countered. 'It was the easy way out, and I took it. It's that simple.'

'The easy way out of what?'

'I lacked direction didn't I?' Anna replied. 'Perhaps I thought marriage would give me a direction, give me something to aim for . . .' she paused, and then said : 'You know the real problem with Keith and me? The fact he wouldn't let us *have* a problem. Anything I wanted, he gave me. I thought he'd grow out of it, once he'd got a good job, got on a bit, but it got worse instead of better. It got so in the end he seemed to agree with everything I said . . . It was like living with an echo . . . Finally, I was saying anything in the hope he'd disagree, learn to think for himself for once. But it was hopeless. He'd just suggest a compromise. That was his answer to everything.'

'He loved you,' Howard said. 'Why else would he give in to you?'

'Because he was . . . weak,' Anna said reluctantly, aware it was a betrayal. 'He even admitted it. He once said I had enough strength for both of us. But I'm not as strong as he thinks.' She looked down at her plate. 'Or I wouldn't have let myself get so irritated by him. You don't know what that kind of irritation is like, Daddy, day in, day out . . . Perhaps that's why I decided to leave him. It was the only way I could prove that one of us could still make an independent decision.'

Howard fell silent, digesting her words. He had always found Keith's sycophantic attitude towards his daughter irritating, but it had never occurred to him that she might share that irritation. However, to Howard, irritation, no matter how severe, was not sufficient grounds to end a marriage.

'Now you've proved your point, you can go back to him, can't you?' he said.

'Daddy...'

'Anyway, you act as though compromising was something to be ashamed of,' he went on. 'Any relationship is based on a compromise, you should have learnt that. Husband and wife, father and son...'

'Father and daughter?' Anna asked wryly.

'I'm letting you stay at home aren't I?' Howard said. 'Even though all my instincts are against it, against what you're doing. What's that if not a compromise?'

'I don't love him, Daddy,' Anna said bluntly. 'I loved him when we first got married, but we were kids then! The trouble is, I've grown up and he hasn't.'

'And where does Emma fit into all this?' Howard asked, deciding to tackle the problem from another direction.

'I didn't want her to witness any more of our silly squabbles,' Anna said with a shrug. 'It wasn't doing her any more good than it was us.'

'Suppose Keith fights you for her?' Howard asked. 'For custody... he might. He'd be within his rights.'

'You forget,' Anna said with a small smile. 'He's used to compromising. He's already said he won't.'

Howard said nothing. Anna glanced at him. 'I wish I could give you neat, pat reasons why I left him, Daddy, but I can't. All I know is I was suffocating, and ever since I left that house, I'd been able to breathe. And if that doesn't make sense, then I'm sorry. But it's the way it is.'

'I see,' Howard said stiffly.

'I'm not expecting you to like what I've done,' Anna continued. 'I know you can't. But accept it. And accept I know what I'm doing.'

'And if I can't?'

'Then say so,' Anna said. 'I can always find somewhere else for Emma and me to stay.'

'In other words, I like it or lump it?' Howard said sharply. 'I'm not in the habit of accepting ultimatums, Anna.'

'I'm not giving you one ...'

'That's what it sounds like to me.' As he spoke, Howard produced his wallet and started to count out some notes. 'Pay the waiter will you? I want to get some air. See if I can't get rid of this headache.' He stood up and reached for his coat. 'You know who I blame for this wretched mess?' he asked, as he pulled the coat on.

'Me, presumably,' Anna replied dully.

'Myself,' Howard answered. 'For never making you work at anything. That's the reason you've always lacked direction, Anna. Because you were never prepared to stick at anything, work at it. Same thing with your marriage. It starts going stale, and you throw in the towel, give up on it.' He started to button his coat. 'That cuts both ways, I'm afraid. So don't be surprised if other people do the same thing with you.' He moved away from the table. 'I'll bring the car round the front.'

Anna watched him thread his way to the door. A sudden gale of uninhibited laughter from the girls at the neighbouring table caused her to turn and look at them. If she could have seen her own face at that moment, she would have read in it, not despair, but a kind of wistfulness that was not far off it.

Later, Anna was to find it difficult to remember the exact sequence of events that followed. She remembered paying the waiter, and pushing her way through the crowded restaurant to the doors, and stepping out into the blindingly bright sunlight. She remembered impatiently waiting, searching the queue of traffic for Howard's car. Exactly when her attention was caught by the small knot of people gathered on the pavement some hundred yards away, she couldn't precisely pinpoint. At first she assumed they were waiting at a bus stop, and dismissed them. But then she dimly perceived that there was no bus stop there. It was at that moment that she recognised Howard's parked car, and she realised it was that which was catching the bystanders' attention. But it was the distant, stubbornly persistent whine of a car horn, which finally triggered her into action. The next thing she could remember was running down the street, towards Howard's car.

He was slumped over the steering column, his head resting against the car horn. A man, looking like a butcher with a grimy, blood-stained white overall, was attempting to lift him out of the driving seat. Anna pushed her way through the small crowd of spectators and hurled herself at the car. She was aware of Howard's grey, inert face, and the blood spattered apron of the butcher, and somehow in her confused mind, she associated the two images. She pushed the man aside, and bent over Howard. His head lolled helplessly on to her shoulder, and his breath was coming out in short, rasping gasps.

A voice, distant, yet familiar, shouted, 'Get someone, a doctor, ambulance . . . Someone !' It was only after the words had been spoken that Anna recognised the voice as her own.

Howard was taken to the casualty unit of St Angela's hospital, and from there he was immediately transferred to the intensive care unit. Helplessly Anna watched as he was examined, undressed, placed on a hospital trolley and wheeled through a labyrinth of corridors to a lift. A nurse gave her his clothes to carry, and, standing beside his trolley in the lift, Anna found herself clutching at them as though it was somehow Howard himself she was clinging to.

Another nurse met them at the lift doors, and issued instructions as the porters pushed him through the heavy swing doors that separated the intensive care unit from the rest of the hospital.

The intensive care ward Sister, sitting at her central observation desk, watched as the nurses and porters transferred the unconscious Howard to a bed, and listened as the nurse from casualty diligently relayed his somewhat scanty case information. Her mind, however, was not so much with the patient at that moment, but with an ashen-faced girl, clutching a handful of clothes, who was standing nearby.

'Who's that?' the Ward Sister whispered.

The casualty nurse, a bespectacled, stolid girl in her early thirties, stopped in mid-stream and turned to follow the Ward Sister's gaze. 'Oh, I think she's the daughter. She's in a bit of a state.' She said it simply, and without sympathy, as if the sight of a distraught relative was an unfortunate aspect of her job, and one she could well do without. She was that type of nurse, conscientious, but unimaginative. The Ward Sister beckoned to Katey Betts, who was passing.

'Doctor Crozier's on his way,' Katey said. 'I just bleeped him.'

'Someone had better see to the daughter,' the Ward Sister replied. 'She looks a bit shaken . . .'

'I was just going to do a B.P. round,' Katey began, and then her eye caught sight of Sarah Lloyd Smith, assisting another nurse attach a drip to Howard's arm. 'How about getting Nurse Smith to look after her?' she suggested. 'I know it's only her first day, but she's got to start somewhere after all . . .'

'All right. But don't let her build up any false hopes, that's all.' The Ward Sister turned back to the casualty nurse. 'She's not to say anything until the doctor's seen him. I don't want anyone thinking we've got a miracle cure. It wouldn't be fair.'

Anna was only dimly aware of the nurses at the other end of the ward. She was too pre-occupied taking in the strange environment around her. The room was large and open plan, with glossy white walls. At first glance it seemed to contain about ten beds, on each one lay an unconscious patient, surrounded by a barrage of complex looking machinery. She watched as the nurses gently transferred Howard to an empty bed. In the casualty unit she had heard a student nurse mutter something about a stroke, and it was only now that the word was starting to take effect. She remembered, as if it was from some other world, that the father of a school friend had suffered a stroke, and been partially paralysed and lost his speech as a result. She had once gone there for tea after school, and he was lying on a sofa in a darkened corner of the sitting-room. She hadn't dared look at him, her embarrassment had been so acute. But after a few minutes of chatting to her friend, she had forgotten he was there. Until he coughed. The normality of it chilled her. She had steeled herself to look over at him. Only his eyes registered anything, clinically observing her across the room. Then, as if the sight of her head wearied him somehow, he closed them, and averted his face, as if he too could dismiss them, as easily as they had him. Such were her thoughts as she looked at Howard's inert face, and she was so pre-occupied with them, that she didn't feel a light touch on her arm, and didn't think to protest as she was led away, into another room.

It was easier than Sarah had expected. Somehow she had expected that when it came to it, she wouldn't be able to find the right words of comfort, but she found she didn't have to think about them. The girl's distress was so obvious, that it triggered off something within her, a compassion which she had almost forgotten she possessed. The girl, she had been told her name was Anna, was still clutching her father's clothes, and gently Sarah took them from her, and lowered her to a seat in the waiting-room.

'I want to stay with him,' Anna said, looking up at her. 'I

have to stay with him . . .'

'Later,' Sarah said. 'You can stay with him later. The doctor is with him now.'

'You don't understand,' Anna said in an oddly flat tone. 'There's something I have to say to him . . .'

'Later. Have a cup of tea first, all right?'

'Mother,' Anna said in the same monotone voice, 'I'll have to ring her, tell her what happened.'

'D'you want me to do it for you?'

Anna looked at her, frowning. Then she shook her head. 'I'll do it. It'll be less of a shock that way.' She stood up. 'Is there a phone anywhere?'

Her mother took the news better than she had dared to hope. At first she had been completely silent, and then she asked what hospital it was. When she got the answer she said : 'I'll be there in ten minutes,' and hung up. It was only then Anna realised her hands were shaking.

When Joan arrived, she was shown into the waiting-room, and they were immediately joined by a doctor. He was young, with a very slight lisp.

'Your husband has a history of heart trouble, I understand?' he said to Joan, after the preliminary introductions.

Joan nodded, and in a quietly restrained voice, started to tell him about Howard's medical background. He had suffered a mild coronary three years before, and been in hospital for over a month.

'And he made a complete recovery?' the doctor asked, writing notes as he spoke.

'He was told to ease off at work,' Joan said vaguely. 'Apart from that . . .'

'And what is his work?'

'He runs a chain of estate agents, south of the river.' Joan's voice automatically took on a note of pride. 'Howard Webster and Son. You may have heard of them?'

The doctor smiled. One of his teeth was chipped, giving

48

him a faintly roguish look. 'I live north of the river.'

'Except there was no son,' Joan went on irrelevantly. 'That was just his joke. He thought it sounded better.' Her control, if that's what it was, was slipping. 'He thought – ' she gulped – 'thought it sounded more impressive for the clients.'

'Mother,' Anna put her hand over Joan's and turned to the doctor, 'he was complaining of a headache all morning. Could that have had anything to do with it?'

'Very likely.' The doctor was about to go on, when Joan interrupted him.

'I *told* him to ease off,' she said, almost accusingly. 'Time and again I told him he was working too hard. But would he listen?'

'When someone has a stroke, Mrs Webster, there are a lot of contributory factors,' the doctor said gently. 'Overwork and strain can be part of it, certainly, but it can also happen for no apparent reason at all . . .'

'All the same,' Joan looked down at her hand, still limply lying in Anna's.

'Look, Mother, if anyone's to blame, it's me. Not you.'

'No one's to blame, all right?' The doctor spoke unintentionally sharply, and they both looked at him in surprise. He softened his manner slightly. He had seen this countless times. Drivers blaming themselves for injuries to passengers, mothers blaming themselves for the illnesses of their babies. Blame, he'd come to realise, was a useless and negative avenue to explore, taking up valuable energy and time, both of which he was critically short of. 'If he's going to get through this,' he went on more gently, 'you're both going to have to help him. So save yourselves for that.'

'Help him?' Anna asked. 'How?'

'By talking to him.'

'I thought he was still unconscious?'

'He is.' The doctor glanced at his watch, and then at the

Ward Sister, standing silently by the door. 'Explain the theory will you, Sister, I'd better get back to him.' He stood up and started to go, then, on an afterthought, turned back. 'And I meant it,' he said. 'What I said about saving your energy. We might all be in for a long wait.'

After he'd gone, the Ward Sister explained what he had meant by 'talking to' Howard. It seemed that there was a new medical approach to intensive care nursing, which involved continually talking to the unconscious patients. Hearing, as the Ward Sister explained to them, was often the first sense to return after unconsciousness, and the sound of a familiar voice often helped stimulate a reaction, which in turn might stimulate the brain.

So Anna and Joan talked to Howard. They took it in turns. They talked about everything and nothing. They talked about the house, the weather, the fact that he hadn't yet put the spring bedding plants out. They talked about Emma, about his work, about the Majorcan holiday that they had always promised themselves. But he still lay behind the thick blanket of unconsciousness.

The afternoon yawned into evening. Anna rang the neighbour who was looking after Emma, and explained that they might not get back that night. After she had rung off she walked down the deserted hospital corridor. By now it was eight o'clock, and it was Joan's turn to be with Howard. Anna was glad of the break. Glad to be out of that silent ward, with the quietly buzzing instruments, and tirelessly efficient nurses. She sat down on a bench in the corridor and thought about her father, and their lunchtime conversation. The fact that it might have been that conversation which in some way had triggered his stroke, weighed heavily on her mind, and as the night wore on, it began to gnaw at her like an obsession. She lowered her head into her hands. She could see his face across that restaurant table, and then the blood-spattered apron of the butcher, as he tried to lever

Howard from the car, and then the two images blended into one, and swam before her eyes. She sat up and tried to blink away the memory. Pinned to the wall opposite her, was a large poster. It depicted a nurse spoon-feeding an elderly patient, and underneath was printed *People remember nurses*. Anna looked at it for a long time, before getting up and returning to the intensive care unit.

There was another relative waiting with them. Mr Wyatt, whose young son had been injured by football hooligans. As Anna came to relieve her mother's vigil by Howard's bed, she could see Mr Wyatt sitting next to his unconscious son, reading from the sports page of a newspaper.

'*And England recruit Brian stepped forward with a well-placed goal. Later, in answer to much muttered speculation about his team's title hopes, he told me: "Where are we now? Fourth? Not all that far behind Manchester City".*' Mr Wyatt broke off, and looked down at his son. 'They'll have to pull their socks up if they reckon on beating Man. City,' he said. 'Either that or start praying for a miracle.' He gazed expectantly at his son's impassive face, as if hoping for some kind of answer. When none was forthcoming he returned to his paper. '*For the Geordies, losing was a certainty. At half-time they were still two goals down . . .*'

Anna turned away. She was filled with a sudden feeling of acute helplessness. Stirred by the sight of this father trying to make contact with his son, she reached out and took Howard's hand. It lay, damp and cold, in her own.

'I'm sorry, Dad,' she said eventually. 'I'll go back to Keith, if that's what you want. Just get better will you? And I'll do whatever you want.' She raised her eyes and looked at her father, but his face still wore the mask of unconsciousness, and she realised that her words were lost on him. She turned the conversation back to small talk. She reminded him of their previous house, and the extension he had designed

51

and built for it, and the garden he had always intended to landscape but never got round to. She sat there idly talking for over half an hour, when suddenly she became aware of a slight humming note from one of the machines next to him. She was about to call someone's attention to it, when two nurses suddenly rushed towards the bed. Before she could protest she was being bundled out of the ward, and as the doors closed behind her she heard one of the nurses shouting into the telephone, 'Cardiac arrest unit? We've an arrest in intensive care, come quickly...'

Despite repeated attempts to resuscitate him, Howard died the following morning. The night nurse reported it to the incoming day nurses, and Sarah, listening to her, felt a sudden stab of loss, almost as though the nurse was telling of the death of someone she knew, rather than that of a total stranger. She thought of Anna, and interrupted the nurse in mid-flow. 'How did they take it?'

The night nurse, an attractive West Indian girl in her early twenties, frowned at her in bewilderment.

'The daughter,' Sarah said, impatiently, 'and his wife?'

'The wife almost seemed to be expecting it . . .' The night nurse said after a moment of consideration. 'But the daughter – ' she hesitated – 'she seemed to blame herself for some reason. Kept on about how it was all her fault. I got the doctor to talk to them, anyway. He sent them both home.' She flipped over the next patient's card. 'Toby Wyatt. Regained consciousness about two am...'

Katey looked at Sarah, standing next to her. She was frowning and chewing her lip.

'You all right?' Katey asked quietly.

Sarah turned to look at her. Then she said in a drained voice: 'It's like you said when I first arrived on the ward, I suppose. Death's just something I'm going to have to get used to.'

'Name of the game, I'm afraid, love,' Katey replied, and then added. 'Still, we didn't lose out completely did we?' Sarah looked at her, puzzled. Katey nodded to the other end of the ward, where Mr Wyatt was sitting next to his son. The boy was sitting up in bed, laughing at some remark of his father's. Sarah regarded them for a moment, and then turned back to Katey. 'No,' she said with a wan smile, 'we didn't lose out completely.'

The funeral was a modest affair. A few of Howard's work colleagues attended, together with some neighbours, and a distant cousin from Wales. Afterwards they all went back to the house for the traditional sherry. It was seven in the evening before Anna closed the door behind the last of them, and returned to join her mother in the sitting-room.

'Thank God that's over,' she said. 'I know they meant well, but why is it people always have to avoid talking about the person who's died at these things?'

'It embarrasses them,' Joan replied tolerantly. 'It's understandable.'

'Perhaps.'

'You should be thinking about collecting Emma from the baby sitter. She'll be wondering what's happened to you.'

'No hurry.' Anna poured a sherry for both of them and sat down by her mother. 'How d'you feel?'

'Numb. How should I feel?'

'You've been fantastic. Everyone said so.'

'I don't know . . .' Joan looked down at her sherry glass, twisting it between her fingers . . . 'I was half expecting it somehow. The way he kept working day and night, never letting up . . . Sometimes it was almost as if he was deliberately trying to kill himself.'

'Daddy?' Anna said incredulously.

Joan glanced at her. 'I don't think you really knew your father at all, Anna. Come to that, I'm not sure anyone did.'

'Except you.'

'Including me,' Joan said simply. She paused, and then went on : 'He wasn't a very . . . affectionate man, Howard. Not what you'd call demonstrative.'

Anna turned away, slightly embarrassed by this sudden unsolicited admission. 'I know,' she said. She didn't know, but she could guess.

'You can't possibly know,' Joan said mildly, as if reading her mind. 'You'd have to be married to him to know that.' She took a sip of sherry. 'What you said in the hospital,' she said after a moment's pause, 'about blaming yourself. You mustn't.'

'Easier said than done, I'm afraid.'

'You heard that doctor. Neither of us is to blame.'

'I can't help it.' Anna stood up and crossed to the window. 'I can't help thinking, if we hadn't had that lunch, hadn't argued the way we did . . .'

'If . . .' Joan said impatiently. 'It's not going to do any good going over old ground, Anna. What's done is done.'

Anna said nothing for a moment, then she slowly turned to face her mother. 'I've decided to go back to Keith,' she said. 'Assuming he'll have me of course.'

Joan stared at her. 'When did you decide that?'

Anna shrugged. 'Does it matter?'

'All right then, *why* did you decide it?' Anna made no reply. 'You must have some reason.'

'Something Daddy said about me being directionless,' Anna said almost reluctantly. 'About how I never stuck at anything. Maybe he had a point.'

'Howard said that?'

'When we had lunch that day.'

'Well, he had no right!' Joan said harshly. 'No right at all.'

Anna looked at her curiously. 'You said it too, remember? When I first came home with Emma, you said . . .'

'Neither of us had the right then,' Jean cut in vehemently. 'Ye gods, if either of us had the courage to do what you're trying to do . . .' She broke off, glanced at Anna, and patted the seat next to her on the sofa.

'Sit down a minute, Anna. I want to say something.'

Curious, yet at the same time inexplicably apprehensive, Anna crossed and sat down next to her.

'Your father and me . . .' Joan hesitated . . . 'Our marriage wasn't all it should have been. We didn't make each other happy, I suppose, it's as simple as that.'

Anna stared at her, bewildered. 'Why didn't you separate?'

'We did,' Joan quickly corrected herself : 'That is, I did. I left him. I packed our bags and took you off to my parents, just as you came to us with Emma. Except, I couldn't go through with it. Finding a job, somewhere to live . . . I couldn't cope with it all. So I took the easy way. I went back.' She paused, took a short gulp of her sherry, and continued : 'He just assumed I'd gone to stay with my parents. And I let him assume it. From that moment, our marriage was based on a lie.' She looked at Anna. 'That's why, when you told us your decision to leave Keith, I appeared to be so against it. I had to be. In condoning your actions, I would have been condemning my own.'

Anna said nothing, and Joan took advantage of her silence.

'If you really are out to prove something to your father, Anna, prove you *can* stick to something. And stick to your decision.'

Anna gave her a look of rueful admiration. 'I'm beginning to think it wasn't only Daddy I didn't know very well.'

Joan didn't reply to that, instead she said : 'I've been thinking about us. About our future. I've a plan, if you'd like to hear it?'

'Go on.'

'I suggest that we sell the house, and get a flat somewhere. I'll look after Emma while you go out to work. Would you like that?'

Anna gave her mother a searching look. She felt a sudden sense of shame. While she had been wallowing in self-recrimination since Howard's death, Joan had been busy planning their future.

'I'd like it,' she said, and as if to close the deal, and bridge the gulf that had always existed between them, she reached out and took her mother's hand.

It was three weeks after the night of the funeral that she saw Sarah Lloyd Smith, while waiting at the bus stop. Seeing her reminded Anna of her feelings of uselessness at the hospital. How she had sat helplessly by and watched, as nurses, girls younger than herself, had attended to Howard. She had been encouraged to talk to him, certainly, but it seemed to her ironic that in the end, it was a stranger who was seeing to his intimate needs, rather than herself. From these vague, dissembled thoughts, the notion to nurse gradually took shape.

It wasn't until over a month later, when an interview had been arranged, that she confided in her mother about the decision. She was expecting suspicion, as if her desire to nurse might in some way atone for Howard's death. But if these thoughts entered Joan's mind, she kept them to herself. To Anna, she simply said, 'What a good idea,' and left it at that.

As the day of the interview grew near, Anna found herself growing increasingly apprehensive. Originally her notion to take up nursing had been made on the spur of the moment, but as the weeks passed, the notion turned into something more tangible. She needed to make a commitment to something, perhaps to replace the void left in her life by Keith, and their failed marriage. Nursing, or so it seemed to her, would not only fulfil her professionally, but emotionally.

The first interview was with the Head of the School of Nursing. It took the form of an informal chat, during which Anna was informed that they had no vacancies for the next term, and that she might have to wait until the following year before they had a place. Anna was more disappointed than she cared to admit, but decided to persevere with her application, and get a temporary job of some kind in the meanwhile. Then, a week after the first interview, she received a letter from the nursing school, stating that they had a cancellation, and would she like to attend another interview, for possible entry in two months? This time, however, she was to be interviewed by the Senior Nursing Officer in the main hospital. Some inner instinct warned Anna that this second interview was more important than the first, and she braced herself for it accordingly.

The Senior Nursing Officer was named Miss L. F. Lewis. Anna, sitting in the outer office, looked at the lettering on the door, and idly speculated as to what the L.F. might stand for. There were two other girls waiting, and the sight of them had increased Anna's nervousness. It hadn't occurred to her that there might be competition for the cancelled place, and any confidence she had managed to muster began to ebb quickly away. She needn't, however, have worried. One of the girls was a qualified nurse in her late twenties, and the other, Brenda Cotteral, a rather shy, diffident teenager from Devon, had already been accepted by the school of nursing, and was simply attending an interview with the Senior Nursing Officer to arrange accommodation in the nurses' home.

Anna's interview started badly and got worse as it went on. Miss L. F. Lewis proved to be a woman in her late middle age, and for the first part of the interview, she asked Anna some routine questions about her background and education. Gradually the space between her questions increased, and in the yawning silence between, Anna felt her tension mounting. Finally, after a particularly long stretch of silence, Miss Lewis laid down her pen and gave Anna a long and candid stare. 'Well,' she said finally, 'let's just run through the details once again shall we? To make sure I've got them right.'

'By all means.'

'You separated from your husband three months ago, with a view to a divorce as soon as it's practicable. Correct?'

Anna nodded.

'And since then you and your little girl have been living with your mother?'

'Yes.'

'And she's agreed to take complete charge of the child while you're at work?'

'That's right, yes.'

'I only ask because as you can imagine, training nurses is very expensive. We have to be sure you wouldn't have to leave half-way through because you haven't made adequate arrangements for your child.'

'She'll be quite taken care of, I promise you.'

'Good. Now then, let's talk about your decision to nurse, shall we?' Miss Lewis went on in a chatty tone. 'Did that come before, or after, your separation from your husband?'

'After,' Anna said. 'I told you, after my separation and after my father died.' She hesitated, and then added: 'Actually I went all through this at my preliminary interview with the nursing school . . .'

'I simply want to be certain that I have the facts in the right order of events, Mrs Newcross.' The use of Anna's married name was somehow disconcertingly formal.

'To be perfectly honest – ' now it was Miss Lewis's turn to hesitate – 'I must confess to being somewhat puzzled by the apparent suddenness of your decision.'

Anna frowned. 'How d'you mean?'

Miss Lewis shuffled the papers on her desk. 'I'm sure I don't have to tell you that nursing is a particularly demanding profession, and consequently needs a particularly strong motivation to enter it.' She gave a sudden, almost sweet smile. 'If one hopes to sustain the course that is . . .' The smile faded almost as quickly as it had come. 'That's why I want to be quite sure you've thoroughly thought out your reasons for wanting to go in for it.'

'I have,' Anna said simply.

'You've come to your decision in rather trying circumstances though, haven't you?' Miss Lewis pointed out. 'Recently separated from your husband, your father dying so suddenly . . .'

'Do the circumstances matter?' Anna asked.

'If they affect the quality of your decision, yes, they do.' She paused briefly and then continued. 'Let's go back a moment, to the time you actually made your decision, shall we? After your father's death you said . . . ?'

'That's right,' Anna replied cautiously.

'Tell me about it,' Miss Lewis said, as if she was addressing a patient rather than a nursing applicant. 'How you felt, what happened . . .'

'He had a stroke,' Anna began. 'And he was taken to your intensive care unit . . .' she shrugged helplessly. 'The following morning he died.'

'And you stayed with him did you? During that time?'

'Yes.'

'Must have been very distressing,' Miss Lewis sounded genuinely sympathetic, and Anna felt her guard lowering.

'It was, yes.'

'Not least, feeling so helpless, having to simply stand by while the experts took over.'

'Exactly,' Anna said. 'Oh, they tried to include us, the nurses and the doctor. Encouraged us to talk to Daddy, in case it helped to trigger a reaction, but it didn't.' She paused. 'I think they were just trying to help *us* actually. Make us feel useful.'

'And did you?'

'Not really,' Anna said truthfully.

'And I suppose that made you feel guilty in turn?' Miss Lewis asked conversationally.

'It's inevitable, isn't it?'

'So you started thinking about taking up nursing?' Miss Lewis asked. 'Perhaps to try and assuage that guilt?'

Anna looked at her sharply, but said nothing.

'It's a fair interpretation of the facts, wouldn't you say?'

'It's one interpretation I suppose,' Anna replied stiffly.

'But not yours?'

'It's *yours*,' Anna said pointedly. 'That's more to the point isn't it?' She could feel a sudden surge of anger, and was helpless to control it. 'I thought you people wanted nurses. I thought there was supposed to be a shortage . . .'

'So there is . . .'

'So how come ever since I set foot in here, you've been trying to cast doubt on my motives?' Anna asked heatedly.

'Establish your motives, Mrs Newcross. There is a difference.'

'Is there?' Anna said bluntly, and then, before she could stop herself, she went on : 'I could have come in here with some neatly worked out bit of patter about how I've always wanted to nurse because I had some divine calling to help suffering mankind. Well, I'm afraid I don't. Maybe I am trying to "assuage my guilt" or however it was you put it. I haven't a clue. All I know is I want a job, and I wanted to do something with a bit more meaning to it than pounding a typewriter all day . . . And if that isn't a good enough "motivation" for you, then I'm sorry. Because it happens to be the only one I've got.' She stood up, aware she was being melodramatic, but too angry and disappointed to care. 'And

I'm also sorry to have taken up so much of your time.' She started for the door, but Miss Lewis's coldly authoritative voice stopped her.

'Mrs Newcross, *I* will decide when this interview is to be terminated.'

Anna turned back. 'There's not much point now, is there?' To her dismay, there was a tremor in her voice.

'As I tried to explain, Mrs Newcross,' Miss Lewis said. 'I simply wanted to establish your motives. And as you so freely admit, yours might not be the most noble in the world, but it has the ring of truth about it if nothing else.' She paused, and a small smile came to her lips. 'And since, as you also admit, it seems to be the only one you've got, it looks like we'll have to make do with it, doesn't it?'

Ten minutes later Anna rejoined Joan and Emma, waiting for her on a park bench opposite the hospital. Joan rose expectantly from her seat : 'Well?'

'I'm in,' Anna said incredulously, and then, in an exhilarated tone, she repeated it : 'I'm *in*.' As she said it, she felt, in one of those unique moments of self-illumination, that at last she might be able to erase the mistakes of the past, and view her future with something she had rarely, if ever, felt. A sense of purpose.

Rebecca Sarah

'For the last time, will you *take* her away?'

The nursery nurse wheeled the trolley bearing the tiny baby nearer the bed.

'This really has gone quite far enough, Mrs Bristow,' she said reprovingly. 'Now I'm going to leave baby here, and you're going to feed her and no more arguments.' She bent over the plastic crib and extended a plump forefinger towards the sleeping baby. 'Little lamb, how could anyone not want to be near you?'

Kathleen Bristow turned dispiritedly away. 'I'll start feeding her tomorrow. All I want to do now is sleep.'

The nursery nurse straightened up. 'Plenty of time for that later,' she said, briskly placing a small bottle of babies' milk on the bedside table. 'Now when she wakes, you're to give her two ounces. And remember to change her nappy before you start the feed . . .' She started to draw back the curtains separating them from the rest of the maternity ward. 'And if she hasn't woken in an hour, you'll have to wake her yourself. Young babies mustn't go longer than five hours without food. It's bad for their digestive system.'

After she had gone, Kathleen hunched herself down in the bed and looked at her .sleeping daughter. She hadn't even thought of a name for her yet, and the omission made her feel guilty. All the other mothers had settled on names the moment their offspring had been born, most had even worked them out during their pregnancies. But Kathleen had scarcely thought about it. I should do, she told herself. If she had a name maybe I'd start thinking of her as a person. Alison? Rebecca? Sally? She didn't really like any of them. She sank back against her pillows. She was *so* tired. No one told you childbirth would take so much out of you. She smiled wryly at her own joke. Take so much out of you . . . Suddenly the sleeping baby gave an involuntary jerk in her sleep, and Kathleen flinched. God, she thought, don't wake up and cry, I couldn't stand it. The baby's eyes fluttered briefly open and then closed, and Kathleen breathed a small sigh of relief. Well if they won't take the baby away from me, she thought, sliding out of bed and reaching for her dressing-gown, I'll just have to take myself away from the baby. She felt for her cigarettes and matches in her dressing-gown pocket, and purposefully started to make her way towards the day room, at the far end of the ward.

'If she's not prepared to give up her career, she shouldn't have had a baby, should she? You can't have it all ways.'

Sarah gritted her teeth and said nothing. She had been working on the maternity ward for nearly a month, and most of that time had been spent in the company of this opinionated nursery nurse. The strain was beginning to tell.

They were sorting out cot blankets in the stock room. The nursery nurse handing up the clean ones, while Sarah, perched on a small step ladder, placed them on shelves.

'Poor little mite . . .' the nursery nurse clucked, 'she didn't ask to come into the world, did she?'

Sarah placed the last blanket on the shelf and scrambled off the ladder.

'Things aren't usually that black and white, are they, Nurse Baverstock.' She hoped that this vague answer might somehow end the conversation, but the nursery nurse was not so easily deterred.

'I might not have had the benefit of all your psychology lectures, love,' she said. 'But I know when a mother feels something for her baby, and that one doesn't. Not a thing.'

Her barbed reference to the psychology lectures was typical, Sarah reflected, as they left the stock room. Nurse Baverstock often made such comments. The training of nursery nurses was fairly basic, less than a quarter of the length of that of an S.R.N. nurse, a fact which constantly galled her. Nurse Baverstock was permanently attached to the maternity ward, which she felt gave her a certain status.

But these S.R.N. students thought they knew it all, just because they had a couple of A-levels and had spent a few weeks stuck in a classroom in the nursing school. What did they *really* know? In the end it was experience which counted, and no amount of training and exams could alter *that*.

Quickly Sarah made her way up the corridor, trying to put as much distance as she could between herself and Nurse Baverstock. She was about to enter the ward, when the Staff Nurse, a likeable, if somewhat pre-occupied, Asian girl in her early twenties, stopped her.

'You were late again this morning, Sarah,' she said distractedly. 'If Sister had been on duty, you'd have been for it, you know that don't you?'

Sarah sighed. It often seemed to her that the nursing profession paid more attention to punctuality than to the actual skill of nursing.

'Only five minutes late. I couldn't help it, the bus didn't come.'

'All the same,' the Staff Nurse's attention was already wandering, 'you'd better watch your step. Sister's getting pretty fed up about it.'

After she'd gone, Sarah made a mental note to report the conversation to her father. She often gave him accounts of such examples of petty discipline, and they would laugh about it together in the evenings. Her father, a senior consultant surgeon at the hospital, shared her own view about many aspects of nursing. He had once remarked that most of the nurses he encountered held the firm belief they could run the hospital single-handed, independent of social workers, doctors, surgeons and anyone else. Such was their humility. She smiled at the memory. What on earth would he say about nursery nurses? But then it was unlikely he had ever come across them. He had often acknowledged that the lower end of the nursing hierarchy was, mercifully, a complete mystery to him. She pushed open the ward doors, and immediately became aware of the high-pitched, almost hysterical note of a baby screaming. An auxiliary nurse hastened towards her.

'It's baby Bristow,' she said anxiously. 'She's howling her head off, and the mother's disappeared somewhere.'

'I'll take care of her,' Sarah said. Panic, panic, panic, that's all they ever seemed to do on this ward. She moved towards Kathleen Bristow's bed. The baby was crying uncontrollably, flaying her little limbs around in the air. Sarah hesitated a moment before picking her up. She still hadn't become used to handling small babies, and always felt a stab of apprehension whenever she approached one. Gingerly she reached into the crib and picked up the baby.

'There now,' she said quietly, aware of a dozen eyes from other beds around the ward watching her. 'What's the matter my love?'

'She's hungry, that's what the matter is.' The voice belonged to a patient in the neighbouring bed. A middle-aged woman who had just had her fourth child, and therefore considered herself to be an expert on the subject of babies.

Sarah ignored her, and reached for the bottle of milk on the bedside table. As soon as the teat neared her mouth, the baby lunged at it, and promptly ceased crying, her whole body contorted with the effort of gulping down the milk. Still holding her, Sarah perched on the side of the bed and glanced idly round. It was mid-afternoon, and most of the patients were preparing themselves for a nap before tea. She looked down at the noisily guzzling baby.

'Where's your Mum got to, I wonder?'

'And what do you think you're doing?'

Sarah looked up to see Nurse Baverstock standing over her, hands on hips, mouth pursed in disapproval.

'I'm feeding her,' she replied quietly. 'What does it look like?'

'I told you, I want the *mother* to feed her,' the nursery nurse said.

Sarah glanced around at the patients, curiously watching them. 'She's not here, is she?'

'You should have looked for her then,' Nurse Baverstock snapped, yanking the baby out of Sarah's grasp. 'She's never going to form a bond with baby if she doesn't feed her, is she?' She took the bottle from Sarah's hand and stuck it into the baby's open mouth. 'Ten to one she's in the day room, smoking. That's where she usually is.'

Sarah opened her mouth to reply, and then closed it. What's the point, she thought. Why sink to her level? She stood up and hurriedly moved away, before the nursery nurse could make any further comments.

Kathleen instinctively hid her cigarette behind her back when the day room door opened. The Ward Sister disapproved of smoking, and made no bones about her feelings on the subject, and Kathleen wasn't in the mood for another lecture. She was relieved when it was only Sarah who entered.

'Don't tell me, my baby's crying again,' she said, as Sarah drew up a chair and sat down next to her. 'Why is it whenever I leave her to get a bit of peace she always chooses that moment to start exercising her lungs?'

Sarah smiled. She liked Kathleen, probably more than any of the other patients. Kathleen Bristow still seemed to be aware that outside the protective walls of the maternity unit there was a world that didn't revolve around her offspring.

'The nursery nurse is feeding her,' she said with a grin. 'And dropping hints like depth charges as to why you aren't doing it.'

'Is she now.' Unconcernedly Kathleen pulled a packet of cigarettes from her dressing-gown pocket, and offered Sarah one. Sarah hesitated, glancing apprehensively at the door.

She was about to refuse when she saw a smile playing round the other girl's lips. 'You can't call your life your own, you nurses, can you?' she said wryly. 'Can't even have a cigarette without fearing the wrath of some Ward Sister coming down on you.'

Sarah stared at her for a moment, then reached out and took the cigarette. 'Never let it be said I don't respond to a challenge,' she said, 'if that's what it was supposed to be?'

Kathleen grinned disarmingly and said nothing, impassively studying Sarah through a haze of blue smoke.

'I like it in here, you know,' she said reflectively. 'There's something illicit about it. Sneaking out of that antiseptic ward to indulge in a thoroughly reprehensible habit like a guilty schoolgirl . . . That's the trouble with making smoking antisocial, exiling us all to some grotty little room like this. They don't realise that some of us actually like being antisocial, that we actually *like* feeling guilty.'

Sarah smiled a mute reply, and for a moment they sat smoking in a relaxed, companionable silence. Then Kathleen leant forward and ground out her cigarette in the ashtray, and almost immediately shook another from the packet and lit it.

'I haven't told you my news, have I?' Her tone was suddenly cautious. 'I'm quitting my job.'

'Quitting it?' Sarah said, surprised. 'But I thought you had it all arranged to go back in a couple of months?'

'I did.' Kathleen blew a thin plume of smoke and watched as it curled its way up to the ceiling. 'But Bob seems to think a mother's place is at home, so . . .' She broke off and glanced at Sarah's puzzled face. 'Bob's my husband, I introduced you, remember?' Sarah nodded, dimly remembering a dark-haired young man in a business suit, simpering over the baby's cot during visiting time the evening before. Kathleen toyed with her cigarette in the ashtray, nudging the ash into small, neat mounds.

'We had a terrible scene about it,' she went on. 'The idea was always that I should go back to work as soon as possible, and we'd get a nanny in. But the second the baby was born, Bob seemed to change his mind. He said it would be unfair on her.'

'It isn't very fair on you though,' Sarah pointed out. 'Making you give up your job if you don't want to.'

Kathleen shrugged indifferently. 'Try telling him that.'

Sarah looked at her curiously. 'Well, I suppose it's not the end of the world,' she said, vaguely feeling she had to make some kind of positive statement. 'You can always return to work later, can't you?'

'It's not that simple,' Kathleen said. 'It's very competitive, commercial art, once you disappear, that's it.' Her tone was suddenly venomous. 'It's taken me six years' hard slog to get where I am, and now Bob wants me to chuck it in without a backward look.' She glanced at Sarah, as if embarrassed at the harshness of her words. 'It's like getting a foothold on an uphill slope, if you lose the foothold, you slip down and never catch up.'

'Don't lose the foothold then,' Sarah said simply. 'Get your nanny and go back to work as you planned.' Kathleen made no reply, and Sarah, instinctively feeling that she needed re-assuring, continued : 'Hundreds of mothers go to work out of choice rather than necessity, and their babies don't suffer do they?'

'I'll bet hundreds of them feel guilty about it as well.'

Sarah frowned. 'Why feel guilty? As long as the baby's taken care of, and given lots of love, what's there to feel guilty about?'

Kathleen abruptly stood up and moved to the window. They were several floors up, and beneath them the afternoon rush-hour traffic was just starting.

'That's just it.' Kathleen leant her forehead against the grimy glass, and looked down at the queue of cars, slowly crawling along the street below her. 'I'm not sure I do love her. I don't hate her . . .' she added quickly, 'it's just that I don't seem to feel anything for her. Not a thing.'

Sarah stared at her. When she had first arrived on the ward she had been warned that sometimes new mothers needed time to learn to love their babies, but now she was actually confronted with it, she was uncertain as to what, if anything, she should say. She was struggling for some suitable comment, when Kathleen spoke again.

'I'm jealous of her, that's partly it, I suppose. Bob's so completely infatuated with her, he can't seem to think of anything else . . . If he knew how I felt . . .' her voice dropped fractionally . . . 'he'd probably hate me.'

'What rubbish !'

'Look, I know what I'm talking about !' Kathleen retorted with sudden anger. 'Because I know Bob. He hasn't an ungenerous bone in his body, so how could he possibly understand something like this?' She moved back to her chair and slumped into it. 'God knows I've tried to feel something for her. I've lain in that bed for hours, staring at her, waiting for something to happen, to feel something. But it was hopeless.' She was fiddling with her cigarette, twirling it frantically between her fingers. 'It was like looking at a stranger.'

'She *is* a stranger,' Sarah said reasonably. 'It takes time for a mother to get to know her baby before she can expect to . . .'

'Spare me the text-book answers, love,' Kathleen interrupted curtly. 'I know all about post-natal depression and the psychology of mother love. Just because I happen to be a woman, it doesn't necessarily follow I'm going to be any good at motherhood, does it?'

A moment of awkward silence followed, broken only by the dull roar of the traffic beneath them.

'Don't you think it's possible . . .' Sarah began, aware she was treading on potentially dangerous ground . . . 'that you

70

feel this way about the baby because you resent her?'

'Resent her? Why on earth should I resent her?'

'Because you've agreed to give up work and look after her. Could it be that?'

'Why should it?' Kathleen irritably flicked some ash from her cigarette. 'It's not *her* fault I have to give up work is it? It's Bob's ...'

'But if she hadn't come along, the question wouldn't have arisen.'

'She's a *baby*, for heaven's sake,' Kathleen cut in. 'I might resent Bob a bit, for going back on our plan, but I certainly don't blame her for it. Give me credit for a bit of intelligence!'

'We're not talking about intelligence, we're talking about emotions,' Sarah said. 'You might not *think* you blame her, but it's inevitable you will a bit, isn't it? I know I would, if I had to sacrifice a successful career. I'm sure you'd feel much better if you went back to work as you originally planned. OK, so you might feel a bit guilty about it, but that's nothing to the guilt you'll feel if you give up everything you've worked so hard for ...'

Kathleen said nothing, and continued to twirl her cigarette between her fingers.

'I think you're reading too much into it,' she said at last. 'Giving up work really has nothing to do with it. I've just got to face the fact that I'm not the doting mother type, and make the best of a bad job.'

'But you've only *been* a mother a few days. You're not giving yourself a chance, Kathleen. You're bound to be a bit confused about how you feel at first, it's a big change in your life. And running away from it won't help, will it?'

Kathleen turned to look at her. 'Who said anything about running away?'

'Isn't that what this business about chucking in your work is all about?' Sarah asked. 'Because you won't face up to your husband and fight for what you really want?'

Kathleen gazed at her for some moments, her mouth moving into a thin, tight line. Suddenly she ground out her half-finished cigarette and stood up.

'The trouble with you nurses,' she said in a cold voice, 'is you think you've got an answer for everything.' She started to head for the door. 'I can hear the tea trolley. All this talking's made me thirsty.'

After she'd left, Sarah went over their conversation in her mind. Perhaps she shouldn't have said that about running away. Kathleen was obviously after approval for her decision, and she should have given it, instead of making her question it. She sighed. Perhaps they were right in the nursing school. Perhaps it *was* better not to get involved in the patients' problems. But then what else did the job have to offer? Dispiritedly she leaned forward and started to stub out the remains of her cigarette, when suddenly the door swung open, and the nursery nurse entered. Quickly Sarah pulled her hand away from the ashtray, but not quickly enough.

'So this is where you've been hiding,' Nurse Baverstock said, staring at the brimming ashtray.

'I was talking to Mrs Bristow.'

'Really?' Nurse Baverstock raised an enquiring eyebrow, wrenching her gaze from the ashtray to look pointedly round the empty room.

'She's just gone back to the ward,' Sarah said, standing up. 'How's her baby?'

'Asleep,' Nurse Baverstock said shortly, and then added, 'I'll have to report you, you realise that?'

'Report me?' Sarah said, genuinely bewildered. 'For what?'

'Smoking on duty. Idling your time in here, when you should be on the ward.'

'I told you,' Sarah said impatiently, 'I was talking to a

patient. You sent me in here to look for her, if you remember?'

'That was a good fifteen minutes ago,' Nurse Baverstock replied. 'I didn't expect you to stay in here and put your feet up.'

'Don't be ridiculous!'

'Do you deny that you've been smoking then?'

'Look!' Sarah said angrily. 'If you want to report me, go right ahead. But I'm not going to let you put me through the third degree. I'm answerable to the Ward Sister, not to you.'

'And you will answer to her, love,' Nurse Baverstock's eyes narrowed malevolently. 'Believe me.' She spun round and went out, banging the door behind her.

Somehow Sarah managed to forget all about the incident. They admitted a Caesarian section from the labour ward, and she was busy for the next hour attending to the new patient and her baby. The mother, a grossly overweight Italian woman in her late thirties, was complainingly coming round from the anaesthetic, when the Staff Nurse entered the curtained off cubicle and drew Sarah to one side.

'I'll take over here. Sister's just come on duty and wants to see you.'

'Where-am-I?' bleated the woman, writhing in her bed. 'Whassa happened?'

'It's all right, love,' Sarah bent over her and placed a restraining hand on her damp shoulder. 'You're in hospital. You've had your baby.'

'My baby?' The woman's eyes flicked open in alarm. 'But he no due yet. He no due for three weeks.'

'It's a she, and she's doing fine.' Sarah turned back to the Staff Nurse. 'Why does she want to see me, do you know?'

'She didn't say.' The Staff Nurse squeezed past Sarah to get nearer the patient. 'But she's in one helluva a mood.'

'He's a she?' The woman was trying to lever herself up in bed. 'But he can't be the she. He can't be.' She dissolved into a flood of noisy tears. 'Mya husband,' she wailed disconsolately, 'he wanta the boy. He no wanta the girl. He wanta the boy!'

'Your husband's tickled pink,' Sarah said. 'He's seen the baby and he's over the moon. So don't worry.'

The woman blinked at her. 'He like the girl?'

Sarah nodded. 'He like,' she said.

The woman sank back against her pillows. 'Ees typical,' she said resentfully. 'We only have the baby because he wanta the boy baby, and now he don't care. All thees trouble, and he don't care!'

The Ward Sister was writing at her desk when Sarah entered the office. Nurse Baverstock sat in the corner, her large arms folded over her ample bosom, gazing fixedly at some distant point out of the window. Sarah closed the door and walked to the desk.

'You wanted to see me, Sister?'

The Ward Sister nodded. 'I'll be with you in a minute.' Sarah stood waiting, uneasily shifting her weight from one foot to another. The Ward Sister was correcting a student nurse's case history, her pen flicking over it with short, violent swirls. Sarah watched for a moment, and her heart sank. The case history the Ward Sister was marking was her own, even upside down she could recognise her untidy writing and the many crossed out words. The Ward Sister lifted her head slightly and caught Sarah's eye.

'Not the tidiest piece of work I've ever had,' she said. She put down her pen and shuffled the papers together. As part of their training, student nurses had to write a case history on one patient in each ward they worked in, and Sarah, as usual, had decided to get it over and done with as early as possible. In the past, this tactic had won her acclaim, as most nurses left it until the last moment. The Ward Sister held out the bundle of papers to her. 'Perhaps you'd like to take it away and read it,' she said. 'We can discuss my comments later.'

'Yes, Sister.' Sarah took the papers and was turning to go, when the Ward Sister stopped her.

'Just a minute, Nurse.'

Resignedly she turned back. In the corner of the room the nursery nurse was examining her nails with sudden, fascinated interest.

'Yes, Sister?'

'I understand you went into the day room this afternoon?'

'Yes, Sister. To look for a patient.'

'I also understand that you spent some considerable time there . . .'

Sarah flicked her eyes over to the nursery nurse and then back to the Ward Sister.

'I was talking to Mrs Bristow,' she said. 'She was in a bit of a state, and I thought . . .'

'What sort of state?'

'She's a bit confused about her feelings towards the baby,' Sarah explained. 'So I tried to talk to her about it.'

'Why didn't you tell one of the senior nurses? The Staff Nurse for example?'

'Since I was on the spot, I thought I might as well try and . . .'

'You know of course that we've all been very concerned about Mrs Bristow and her lack of feelings about her baby,' the Ward Sister interjected. 'And that she's to see the psychiatrist about it before she's discharged?'

'As it happens, I didn't know that, no.'

'In that case,' the Ward Sister continued evenly, 'perhaps you'll remember me telling the nurses not to talk to her at any length about the problem, because the psychiatrist doesn't want anyone confusing the issue before he sees her?'

'I don't see how talking to her can do any harm,' Sarah said indignantly. 'And anyway, I don't remember you saying anything about the psychiatrist at all.'

'I said it at report yesterday morning, and again at the teach-in in the afternoon.'

'I'm sorry, but I don't remember it.'

'Perhaps you weren't listening.' The Ward Sister's tone was mild, rather than accusatory. 'You do seem to let your attention wander rather, don't you?'

Sarah decided it was prudent to say nothing.

'Anyway, that isn't why I wanted to see you.' The Ward Sister leant back in her chair, her eyes scanning Sarah's face. She was in her early forties, with short cropped hair, and a decisive, angular face. 'I understand you were smoking in the day room.'

Sarah glanced once again at Nurse Baverstock, who lifted her eyes and stared back at her unblinkingly.

'I had a cigarette, yes.'

'It doesn't matter that you had only the one, Nurse. What's important is that you had any at all.'

'She was smoking, Mrs Bristow that is, and I thought it would seem more sociable if I joined her.'

'I'm not interested in why you did it,' the Ward Sister said. 'You know the rules on the subject, and yet you flagrantly broke them.'

Sarah sighed. What would her father say when she reported this conversation to him? He would probably make some remark about rules being made to be broken, particularly when the rule was so tediously petty, as this one clearly was.

'You know how anxious we are to discourage smoking among the patients,' the Ward Sister said. 'And you go and set them an example like this.'

'But Mrs Bristow already smokes, Sister.'

'Which means she doesn't need encouraging,' the Ward Sister snapped. 'If you'd refused to have one, it might have made her reconsider the habit herself.'

Sarah shot a baleful look at the nursery nurse. 'Very well,' she said grudgingly. 'I'm sorry. But the whole reason I went into the day room is because Mrs Bristow was hiding there to get away from her baby. It's obvious she can't cope with her yet, but certain people keep shoving the baby by her bed anyway. I can't see how that's going to help the psychiatrist either. It just makes the patient feel more guilty than she already does.'

'We're not here to talk about the whys and wherefores,' the Ward Sister replied. 'We're here to talk about you, and your attitude to your work since you came on this ward.' She broke off and turned to Nurse Baverstock. 'You'd better get back to the nursery. I'll deal with this now.'

'As you like, Sister.' Nurse Baverstock hauled herself up and started for the door. 'Thank you for your time.'

Sarah winced at the sycophantic tone in Nurse Baverstock's voice, and watched in relief as the door closed behind her.

'I took the liberty,' the Ward Sister was speaking again, 'of getting some of the other Ward Sisters' reports on you, to see if they concurred with my own view.' She started fumbling through some papers on her desk. 'Unfortunately it seems they do.' She looked up at Sarah. 'You seem to find great difficulty in obeying even the most routine aspects of procedure, for example . . .' she glanced down at the papers . . . 'you seem to have been repeatedly pulled up about impunctuality, about your uniform, about carelessly presented written work . . . The list is endless.' She pushed the papers to one side. 'It's as if you seem to believe yourself to be above such things.'

Sarah said nothing. The Ward Sister was gazing at her, as if hoping for some kind of response. She'll have a long wait, Sarah thought sullenly, I have absolutely no intention of behaving like a guilty schoolgirl.

'I realise your father is the consultant surgeon here,' the Ward Sister said at last. 'And it's possible that you think this gives you some kind of elevated status, but it wouldn't matter if your father were only a porter. I cannot tolerate any more of your careless attitude. You're not pulling your weight, and it's not fair, either to the other nurses or the patients.'

Sarah felt a flood of angry colour come into her cheeks at the mention of her father. The Ward Sister seemed not to notice however.

'Now either you think again and start to behave responsibly, or I'm afraid I'll have to ask the nursing tutor to take you off my ward.' She paused and then added : 'I haven't got room for passengers.'

'All because I was caught smoking in the day room?'

'The actual incident is unimportant, Nurse. As I told you, it's just one in a long line of examples of your attitude.'

'I don't think it's *my* attitude that's at fault at all,' Sarah said angrily. 'If my father really were just a porter, you'd bend over backwards to help me. As it is, you can't wait to . . .' she broke off, searching for the right word, 'pick on me,' she ended lamely.

'Don't be absurd !'

'I haven't seen any of the other students being hauled up in front of you.'

'Perhaps they don't deserve it.'

'And what about that nursery nurse?' Sarah demanded. 'She may not break any rules, but she's no better for it. Disturbing sleeping babies to weigh them, making the mothers keep them on the ward all night, even if they're exhausted . . .'

'That's enough !' Now it was the Ward Sister's turn to be angry. 'Trying to blame someone else won't get you anywhere, and you're just letting yourself down by doing it.'

'I'm simply trying to point out,' Sarah said helplessly, 'that sticking to the rules doesn't necessarily make you a good nurse . . .'

'I think I know what qualifications make a good nurse,' the Ward Sister said thinly. 'Perhaps better than you.' She stood up. 'I'm not prepared to argue, I've got a ward of patients to see to. I want to see a marked improvement in your attitude, or I'll have to get on to your nursing tutor. I hope I make myself clear.' She headed for the door, and then turned back. 'And don't think that all we've been talking about is the fact you were caught smoking. That's only a symptom of your feelings about the job. And I don't have to tell you that it's no earthly good clearing up symptoms, if the patient is still ill. That's simply a disguise, not a cure.'

Sarah stared at her for a moment. 'Suppose a patient doesn't acknowledge there's anything wrong with her?' she asked at last. 'And therefore doesn't want to be cured, what then?'

The Ward Sister hesitated before replying. 'Then I don't know what she's doing in a hospital,' she said, and left the room.

At what precise moment it occurred to Sarah to stage her walk-out, she couldn't later remember. She had gone back to the ward, fully intending to resume her duties, when she had encountered Nurse Baverstock, gloating with barely concealed triumph.

'Baby Newman needs changing, if you think you can manage it. I'm going to do a milk round,' and she trundled off, pushing a trolley of bobbing bottles in front of her. For a second Sarah sullenly watched her retreating figure, and then quite suddenly found her feet moving in the opposite direction. Shove it, she said to herself, as she headed towards the locker room at the end of the ward corridor. Shove *all* of it. The job, the Ward Sister, the nursery nurse, the rules, the *lot* of it. If all nursing came down to was punctuality and petty discipline, she was well out of it. Seething with self-righteous indignation, she took off her uniform, climbed into her jeans, and walked out of the hospital without a backward glance.

Sarah lived with her parents in a spacious mansion flat overlooking the river. As she rattled up in the lift she found herself praying no one was in, and on entering the flat, promptly called out to her mother. But silence greeted her, so she gratefully headed towards the bathroom, and started to run a bath. A few minutes later, as she lay wallowing luxuriously in the hot water, she went over the events of the day, and speculated on how her mother would react to her throwing in nursing. Maybe she should wait until her father came home to tell her story. Her mother was the direct opposite from her father. Max indulged his daughter unashamedly, and Sarah naturally gravitated towards him. As far as he was concerned, Sarah was still a child who should have a chance to enjoy herself before thinking seriously about anything.

Sarah's mother, who had given up her own hard-won career as a doctor when Sarah was born, was the ambitious member of the family. Liz had been behind Max all the way as he climbed the hospital hierarchy. It was she who had encouraged him to read the medical journals and apply for strategic posts, and she had been equally ambitious for Sarah. Her dream of being mother to a doctor had been shattered when Sarah's A-level results came through. No medical school would have accepted her, despite all her father's influence. But instead of backing up Liz in encouraging Sarah to try again, Max had financed a six-months jaunt round Europe. Then Sarah had drifted from one clerical job to another, until she astounded both her parents by deciding to enrol as a student nurse at St Angela's. Liz was surprised that at last Sarah seemed to be interested in something other than her social life, but she soon realised that Sarah's attitude to nursing was as casual as ever. She never stopped complaining about the discipline, the pettiness of her tutors and nearly every other aspect of her training. Worse, her father encouraged her, and at night they would often laugh together at the behaviour of the senior nurses and tutors.

Remembering her mother's grim disapproval, Sarah knew she'd get no sympathy *there* if she told her she had walked out on the job. She had finished her bath, and was rummaging in the fridge for something to eat, when she heard the front door opening, and her mother's familiar tread. Sarah froze and listened as the footsteps grew nearer. The kitchen door swung open and her mother entered, her arms full of bags of groceries.

'Goodness, you startled me,' she said as she lowered the bags on to the kitchen table and looked at her daughter. 'I wasn't expecting you home until at least seven. It's not your half day again is it?'

'No . . .' Sarah hesitated. Oh, tell her, she said to herself, and get it done with. She took a breath.

'As a matter of fact,' she began casually, 'I'm home early because I've packed it in.'

Her mother paused in unpacking the grocery bags and looked at her blankly. 'Packed it in? Packed what in?'

'Nursing,' Sarah said. 'Some tedious nursery nurse reported me for . . .'

'What d'you mean, packed it in?' her mother interrupted. 'You mean you've just walked out?'

'More or less.'

'Why, for God's sake?'

'Because I'm sick of it, Mother. I'm sick of their petty rules and regulations, and sick of . . .'

'So you just walk out, without a word to anyone?'

'I'm going to put my resignation in writing, but it won't

make any difference. I've made up my mind.'

Liz sank to a chair and gazed at her daughter.

'Well, you'll just have to unmake it then, won't you?' she said at last. 'Where's your uniform?'

'In the locker room by the ward, why?'

Her mother ignored the question and asked another. 'And exactly when did you stage this magnificent "walk out"?'

Sarah shrugged. 'I don't know. An hour ago . . .'

'Right, well get your coat. I'm driving you back there. If you're quick it's possible no one's missed you. You can pretend you've been on some errand . . .'

'I don't think you heard me, Mother,' Sarah said. 'I'm finished with it. *Finito*. And I have absolutely no intention of setting foot in the place again, so you'd be wasting your time trying to make me.'

Liz didn't speak for a moment, still watching Sarah's face. Finally she roused herself and stood up. 'We'll see about that,' she said. 'We'll see what your father has to say about that.'

Sarah smiled. 'All right. But I think we both know what he'll say, don't we?' For a second mother and daughter looked challengingly at each other across the room.

'You're very sure of him, aren't you?' Liz said.

'Over something like this . . .' Sarah nodded, 'yes, I am.'

'You think he'll back you?'

'I know he will. You've heard him on the subject of nurses. His opinion of them is even lower than mine.'

'That's just big talk and you know it. All consultants talk like that, they don't mean it.'

'Look, I'm not knocking nursing, Mother,' Sarah said impatiently. 'I think it's great, if you're the sort of person who's prepared to put up with all the rubbish that goes with it. And I'm not, it's that simple.'

Her mother didn't speak for a moment, and when she did her tone was flat and devoid of expression.

'If your father asked you to go back, would you do it?'

'He won't.'

'But if he did?'

'I don't know . . .' Sarah frowned. 'Why would he want me to? He always lets me decide these things for myself.'

'But if he decided you should go back, you'd abide by what he said?' Her mother was obviously determined to press the point, and Sarah finally nodded.

'I suppose so . . .'

'That's all I wanted to know.' Liz opened the door and was leaving the room when Sarah stopped her.

'I think you're forgetting something, Mother. After walking out like that, I doubt they'd let me go back, even if I begged them on my hands and knees.'

'I can't see you doing that,' Liz said, 'you wouldn't know where to begin would you?' And she went out, leaving Sarah with the vaguely uncomfortable feeling that the evening ahead was going to prove more troublesome than she had expected.

It was eight o'clock before Max came home, and Liz was waiting for him in the sitting-room. He threw himself into his favourite fireside seat, while she mixed him a gin and listened to his account of his day. Even though she was anxious to tell him about Sarah's news, she listened diligently. Max's nightly unwinding ritual never altered. It consisted of sipping his gin and tonic and filling in Liz on the details of his various patients, conversations he'd had, decisions he'd made, decisions he'd postponed, until at last the tapestry of his day lay before her, ready for her judgement.

Liz was more than a sounding board to Max, she was his conscience. Often he was glad to incur her reproach, because he felt it somehow absolved him of the blame over a possible mistake in diagnosis or treatment. At other times he was equally anxious for her approval, as if the rightness of a particular decision could only be confirmed when she had praised him for acting correctly. Tonight's ritual was no exception, and he was surprised when she made no comment to his soliloquy.

'You're very quiet, old girl,' he said, looking at her over the top of his glass. 'Had a bad day?'

'Pretty ghastly, yes.'

'Poor old love.' He stretched out, savouring the external warmth of the fire, and the internal warmth of the alcohol. 'Here I am, moaning on about my problems without a thought for yours.'

'It isn't my problems I'm thinking about,' Liz said. 'It's Sarah's.'

He looked at her enquiringly. 'What's she been up to now?'

Quietly and undramatically Liz told him about Sarah's actions that afternoon, and their subsequent conversation.

'Where is she now?' Max asked, after she had finished.

'In her room. I asked her to stay there until we'd had a chance to talk.' Liz hesitated before going on. 'And I also asked her if she would abide by your decision as to whether or not she should go back, and she agreed.'

'My decision?'

'That's right.'

'It's a bit late for *me* to decide anything isn't it?' Max asked. 'It looks as though she's already decided things for herself.'

'I want your support on this, Max,' Liz said quietly. 'I want you to tell her to go back.'

Max stared at his wife, surprised at the grim tone in her voice. 'It's not worth turning this into a family feud,' he said. 'The girl's twenty-two, if she wants to chuck it in, it's up to her, isn't it?'

'No, Max, it isn't!' Liz was practically shouting now.

Abruptly she stood up and moved over to the mantelpiece to stand in front of Max. 'For years I've tried to get Sarah to settle down into some kind of career, and for years you've been telling me that she's still a child, and there's plenty of time for that later. Yet now you say she's old enough to make her own decisions! Well it's time I told *you* something, Max. Ever since Sarah was born you've spoilt and indulged her . . .'

Max attempted to interrupt, but she ploughed on. 'Yes you have! You've given in to her on everything. If you'd backed me before she might have been at medical school by now, but no, instead of trying to make her study for her exams, you let her gallivant off to parties every night . . .'

'If she'd wanted to go to medical school she would have studied for the exams, wouldn't she?' Max rejoined. 'She didn't want to go, it's obvious.'

'That's the whole point, Max,' Liz said wearily. 'She doesn't know *what* she wants, can't you see? And if she doesn't know what she wants, it's up to her parents to guide her towards what she *needs,* isn't it? And what the girl needs is a career. She's too intelligent to drift aimlessly from job to job, and you know it.'

Max didn't answer at once. He frowned and then leaned forward to place his empty glass on the table beside him.

'Since we're obviously having a truth session,' he said at last, 'we may as well lay all our cards on the table. The reason you're so anxious for Sarah to have a career, is because you had to give up your own when she was born. Something you've never forgiven her for.'

'Nonsense!'

'Is it?' He looked up at her. 'Well, if I have indulged her, it's because I've been trying to fill in the gap, Liz. The gap you leave, because you won't show her any affection.'

Liz averted her eyes. 'If I do resent her,' she said quietly, so quietly he had to strain to hear her. 'It's not simply be-

cause of my career, it's because of the way she's come between us. Besides . . .' she turned to face him again . . .
'there are other ways of showing affection besides your way.
One way of showing you love a child is by trying to help
her develop some kind of purpose, to show her she *can't* have
everything just for the asking, and that running away when
the going gets rough does more harm than good.'

'Who says she's running away?'

'She's thrown in her job hasn't she? It's exactly like the
way she ran off abroad after the fiasco of her A-levels. She
just can't face up to life as it really is, and the reason she
can't, Max . . .' she paused, and looked him full in the
face . . . 'is because you encourage her not to! You tell her
what she wants to hear, because you're afraid if you don't
she might love you less. Well, I'm prepared to risk that, because I know in the long run, that isn't what's important.
What's important is that I love her enough to tell her when
she's making a mistake, even if it does make me unpopular.'
She stooped to pick up his glass from the table and started
for the door, then, as if on an afterthought, she paused and
turned back. 'I don't know why she decided to take up nursing. It was the last kind of job I expected her to choose. I
thought she'd opt for something much less demanding, but
she did opt for it, and I think she had a reason. She wanted
to test herself, to see if she was up to it. And if you let her
chuck it in now, she'll never know if she could have made it
or not. Well, I'm certain she is up to it, Max, and I want you
to help me make her prove it. If not to us, to herself.'

Outside in the hall, Sarah felt numb. A few minutes earlier,
hearing her parents' raised voices, and knowing she was the
cause, she had left the sanctuary of her room intending to
intervene. She had been about to open the sitting-room door
when she had suddenly paused. Liz was telling her father
what had happened, and Sarah found herself listening. Her

mother's last words stunned her. Over the years Sarah had learnt to turn to Max for affection. She had simply assumed that Liz had a less affectionate nature than her father, and left it at that. Now she was confronted with a different image of her mother. She realised, for the first time, the genuine kind of love Liz had for her. She felt a sudden stab of shame. Not only had she underrated her mother, but she had vastly overrated Max. He had always given in to her, she realised ruefully, because it was an easy way of ensuring his daughter's affection. Her mother, on the other hand, was thinking about Sarah's future. And Sarah discovered something else as she stood in that draughty hall. Her mother knew her better than she even knew herself. She realised it was true, she *had* gone into nursing to put some kind of measure on her capabilities, which previously, thanks to Max constantly indulging her every whim, had never been put to the test. The thought occurred to her that if she chucked in nursing now, she would have failed that test. Even as the thought crossed her mind, she could hear Liz moving towards the sitting-room door, and quickly she darted back into her room.

A few minutes later, having sufficiently composed herself, she emerged, and found Liz in the kitchen preparing a cold supper for Max. Liz glanced up at her as she entered, and then lowered her eyes.

'Your father wants to talk to you. He's in the sitting-room.'

Sarah pulled out a chair and sat down. 'I don't have to talk to him, Mother,' she said. 'I've thought it over and . . .' She paused, searching for the right words. Sarah was not used to climbing down, and suddenly found it difficult to express herself. 'Well, the fact is, I've reconsidered it,' she said bluntly. 'I'm going back to the hospital tomorrow.'

Liz stared at her. 'Why . . . ? What made you change your mind?'

Sarah shrugged. 'Let's say I took a long, hard look at myself, that's all. There's a lot I don't like about nursing, an awful lot. All the senseless petty rules and . . . But there's also a lot I *do* like, and I suppose I've got to take the good with the bad, like everyone else.'

Liz didn't speak for a moment, but merely stood, staring at her daughter. Sarah, looking back at her, saw in her expression a kind of respect she couldn't remember seeing before. For her part Liz, looking into the younger face of her daughter, saw a similar kind of respect, a respect she couldn't guess the reason for, but welcomed nonetheless.

Going back to the hospital wasn't as easy as Sarah had anticipated. On hearing her decision, Max had suggested that he ring the nursing tutor and smooth the way for her, but Sarah had vehemently declined his offer, saying she must face the full consequences of her actions. The following morning, she went to see the nursing tutor who interrogated her for nearly an hour as to firstly, why she had left the ward in such a high-handed, irresponsible manner, and secondly, why she had suddenly decided to return. Something in Sarah's contrite replies seemed to mollify her anger however, and after a ten-minute diatribe on Sarah's inexcusable behaviour, she rang the sister of the maternity ward, and gained her reluctant consent to let Sarah return.

As soon as Sarah entered the ward, one of the nurses told her that Ward Sister was waiting to see her, and Sarah braced herself for another attack. The Ward Sister was in the clinical room, sorting out boxes of freshly-delivered dressings packs. On seeing Sarah, she asked the auxiliary helping her to leave them, and closed the door behind her.

'When you walked out of my ward yesterday,' she said, leaning against the door and looking at Sarah across the room, 'I swore I'd never let you set foot in it again.'

Sarah, sensing something else was coming, dropped her

eyes and said nothing.

'I don't know what your reasons are,' the Ward Sister continued, 'and I'm not interested. As far as I'm concerned any girl who behaves like that, isn't worthy of nursing. It's that simple. And if there's any repetition of that kind of behaviour, any repetition at all, your feet won't touch the ground. Do you understand?'

'Yes, Sister.'

'Very well.' She moved away from the door. 'You may return to your duties.'

'Thank you, Sister.' Sarah turned to go, and then paused : 'Sister?'

The Ward Sister, who had returned to her boxes of dressings packs, looked up at her.

'Why *did* you decide to let me come back?'

The Ward Sister hesitated briefly before replying. 'Kathleen Bristow,' she said. 'Whatever you said to her yesterday in that day room did the trick. She had a tremendous showdown with her husband during visiting time, and ever since then we haven't been able to prise her and the baby apart. She's a totally different person.' She looked at Sarah curiously. 'Just what *did* you say to her?'

'Only that I thought she'd regret giving up her job,' Sarah replied. 'And that she should persuade her husband to let her carry on with it.'

The Ward Sister pulled out a stool from under the work bench, and sat down. 'I didn't even know she planned on giving up her work,' she said ruefully. 'Come to that, I didn't even know she worked at all.' She glanced at Sarah. 'It's very easy to lose touch with the patients when you're running a ward.' She paused, and then added : 'I suppose that's how you came to know about it? By talking to her over a cigarette in the day room?'

'I suppose it is, yes.'

'H'mm.' The Ward Sister gazed at her thoughtfully,

absently chewing on her lower lip. 'Well,' she said at last, 'next time a patient confides in you, I'd be glad if you told me about it. I'm just as anxious to help as you are, you know.' She stood up and went back to the box of dressings packs. 'And next time you think one of them has a problem,' she added, as Sarah opened the door, 'try talking about it over a fruit gum rather than a cigarette. Then the nursery nurses won't find it quite so easy to complain about you.'

Back on the ward, the first person Sarah encountered was Nurse Baverstock, who wasted no time to jibe at her. 'Well, well,' she said, pulling up in front of Sarah and regarding her with folded arms, 'so the prodigal returns! But for how long, that's the question.'

Sarah gave her a sweet smile. 'For as long as you want to keep dishing it out, love,' she said. 'Now if you'll excuse me, there's a patient I'd like to see.' And quickly she squeezed past and walked down the ward towards Kathleen Bristow's bed. Kathleen was absorbed with feeding her baby, and wasn't aware of Sarah until she drew up a chair and sat down beside her.

'Hello,' she said, greeting her with a radiant smile. 'I've been dying for you to get back on duty.'

'So what's all this about a showdown with your old man?' Sarah asked.

Kathleen's face fell. 'I wanted to tell you about it myself,' she said reproachfully, and then smiled. 'Oh well, at least I can thank you, that's the important thing. I did just as you said, I thought it over and decided maybe you had a point. So I told Bob I wanted to go back to work. He didn't agree of course, and we argued about it during the whole of visiting time. But he finally saw my side of things, and ever since then . . .' she shrugged . . . 'instead of dreading the future, I've been looking forward to it. And as for this little thing . . .' she looked down tenderly at the baby in her arms . . . 'if I ever did resent her, I've certainly stopped now.' She kissed the baby's forehead. 'I've even thought of a name for you, haven't I ?'

'And not before time,' Sarah said, in a tone of mock reproof. 'What is it ?'

Kathleen looked at her. 'Rebecca,' she said, smiling. 'Rebecca Sarah Bristow.'

A Shadow of Doubt

Dear Mummy and Daddy,

Thank you for your letters. I'm sorry if I've worried you by not writing back for so long, but several things have happened to me and . . .

Brenda hesitated, her pen poised over the notepaper. She lowered it and moved restlessly over to the window. The nurses' home was situated directly opposite the main hospital block, divided by a small concrete quadrangle. Brenda stood at the window, gazing absently down at the stream of people emerging from the entrance to the hospital. Some of them she recognised, nurses coming off duty and gratefully heading towards their rooms in the nurses' home; others were less familiar, porters scurrying self-importantly off on some errand; bewildered visitors with bunches of flowers, following the maze of signs to far-flung wards; white-coated doctors purposefully striding from one department to another.

When Brenda had first arrived three months before, the view from her room in the nurses' home had depressed her unutterably. She was used to seeing an expanse of green fields and trees from her window, and the relentless bulk of the grey-bricked hospital block dismayed her. But in time she found herself growing increasingly fond of it. She would spend evenings looking through the bright, curtainless windows of the hospital, watching the perpetual motion of activity inside. Nurses weaving their way between beds, patients shuffling down the ward, doctors ruminating over clipboards. The sight of it somehow comforted Brenda, it was like watching a performance on a stage, and knowing that she had a part, however small, to play in it. She rested her head against the cold surface of the window. Looking back, the events of the past weeks seemed like a play as well. Had they really happened? Or had she dreamt the whole thing? She returned to her unfinished letter. Should she tell her parents about it, she pondered, and would they understand if she did? She had to tell *someone*, she knew that. She picked up her pen. Perhaps if she wrote it all down, in the exact sequence it had happened, she could expiate it, as one often expiated a bad dream, simply by relating it. She sighed, well it was worth a try anyway, and she cast her mind back to eight weeks before, and started to write.

It had all started one Friday afternoon. She was in the clinical room with Staff Nurse, sorting out the drugs trolley. The Staff Nurse's name was Barbara Holmes, and ever since Brenda's arrival on the female medical ward from the school of nursing, she had been in awe of her. Barbara was a tall, rather horsey girl who kept herself to herself. She wore pale-blue tinted glasses, and Brenda finally decided it was these, rather than the girl herself, which disconcerted her. Brenda would make a remark, and the bespectacled face would turn in her direction, and the mouth would reply. But the eyes, obscured behind the two ovals of blue glass, revealed nothing. Brenda consequently preferred to say nothing rather than provoke another silent scrutiny from behind the blue lenses. As a result they had worked for the best part of a quarter of an hour in virtual silence, broken only by the occasional scratching of Barbara's pen as she noted down what drugs they were short of, and what needed re-ordering. The whole procedure surrounding drugs intimidated Brenda. The drugs trolley was a kind of wooden box on wheels, which the qualified nurses (students weren't allowed to handle drugs) pushed around the ward. The trolley contained no dangerous drugs, which were kept separately in a cupboard in the clinical room; the drugs trolley, like the drugs cupboard, was always locked when not in use, and the keys were held by either the Staff Nurse or Sister on duty.

Many of the drugs' names were still a complete mystery to Brenda, and the task of learning them, and exactly what function they performed, was not made any easier by the fact that experienced nurses often referred to drugs by both their trade and pharmaceutical names. At first Brenda had screwed up her courage sufficiently to ask the Staff Nurse what a particular drug did, and what it was called, but the abrupt manner of Barbara's answers had deterred her from continuing. She finally gave up, making a mental note to look up some of the more complex drugs and their uses later.

It was into this atmosphere of quiet concentration that Robin intruded. He was a medical student in his third year, and made frequent visits to the ward to follow up various cases he was studying. Brenda was aware of a change in herself whenever she saw him. She would automatically hold herself more upright and pull her tummy in, as if hoping a veneer of outward composure might conceal her inner confusion. And confuse her he certainly did. She would just have to glimpse him, and her heart would start violently thumping and her hands shaking. She had often, unsuccessfully, tried to analyse why he should have this effect on her. He was too tall and angular to be considered good-looking in the traditional sense, in some ways he reminded her of her elder brother, Mark. He had the same brash confidence and the same winning way, as if he regarded his popularity to be a right, rather than a privilege. Robin was now leaning against the door frame, talking about a patient's file that had gone astray. Feeling Brenda's eyes on him, he glanced at her, and she felt her cheeks reddening and cursed herself. She busied herself with checking a label on a bottle of pills and became aware that the Staff Nurse was addressing her.

'Perhaps you could find it, Nurse?'

Brenda looked into the two bland ovals of blue glass. 'I'm sorry?'

'Mrs Abbot's case file. See if it's in the office will you?'

'Yes, Staff.'

Brenda replaced the pill bottle and headed for the door. Robin didn't attempt to move when she got there, and as she squeezed by she could feel his breath on her face, and through the thudding in her ears, she heard him say, 'Thanks, that's nice of you.'

It only took a second for her to find the file in the Sister's office, and she quickly picked it up and made her way back to the clinical room.

She was to go over the sight she saw next at least a hundred times. The Staff Nurse was at the sink, with her back to the door, and the drugs trolley was open behind her. Robin, no longer lounging in the doorway, was next to the trolley, and as Brenda turned into the room, she saw his hand dart into the drugs trolley. In one motion the hand levered off the cap from a pill bottle, shook a few pills out, returned the cap on the bottle, and then dived back into his overall pocket. It all happened so quickly that it took Brenda a second to actually register what she saw. Then Robin turned and caught sight of her. His whole manner altered at the expression in her eyes. His startled face purpled and then puckered into alarm. He suddenly struck Brenda, not as a confident young man, but a guilty child. She wrenched her eyes away and looked at the Staff Nurse, still busy at the sink.

'Staff?'

She heard him catch his breath and she glanced swiftly back at him. The guilt was still there, but there was something else replacing it. A kind of intensely beseeching look, which was more powerful than any words he might have spoken. Brenda made her decision instantly. She knew she should report what she had seen, but those hungry, anxious eyes staring at her across the room were suddenly more important than any sense of duty. The Staff Nurse turned to her and she held out the file.

'Is this the one?'

'Does it say Mrs Abbot on it?' There was a faintly impatient note in the Staff Nurse's voice.

96

'Yes.'

'Then it's obviously the one isn't it?' The Staff Nurse turned back to the sink. Brenda forced herself to face Robin. Silently he took the folder out of her hands and started for the door. When he reached it he paused and looked at her over his shoulder and said just one word : 'Thanks.'

After he'd gone Brenda surreptitiously checked the pill bottle. They were amphetamines, sometimes given to patients to relieve depression and give them energy. She breathed a sigh of relief that at least they were nothing more harmful. Then another thought occurred to her. Why did he want them? If he needed amphetamines why not go to his own doctor instead of stealing them from the ward? And then, more disturbingly, other thoughts crowded into her head. Why *had* she covered for him like that? Was it simply compassion or was she trying to win his favour? And what would be the consequences? If it came out she had deliberately kept quiet, she could be regarded as an accessory. Accessory. She shuddered at the word and the ugly picture it evoked. But supposing she told the Staff Nurse what she'd seen? What kind of trouble would *he* be in? All these questions, and more, filled her mind during the afternoon. Too dazed to concentrate on her work, she found herself making silly mistakes; and all the time her eyes probed the ward, seeking him out, although what she would have said if she had seen him, she didn't know. As it happened, he took the initiative. He was waiting for her in the hospital corridor when she came off duty. At first she didn't see him, and only became aware of him when he fell into step beside her.

'I want to talk to you,' he glanced around and dropped his voice to a whisper. 'You haven't said anything have you?'

She looked at him and slowly shook her head. He smiled in relief.

'I'd like to explain, if you'll give me the chance?'

D

'I think perhaps you'd better.'

'Are you free tonight? I thought perhaps we could go out somewhere. There's a pub I know by the river, do you fancy it?'

'If you like. I'll have to change first.'

He nodded distractedly. 'I'll meet you in the forecourt. In half an hour.' Without waiting for her confirmation, he was gone, lost among the other hospital staff, swarming homewards down the corridor.

The pub was noisy and crowded, and they had difficulty getting a seat. For the first few minutes they stood by the bar, shouting awkward small talk at each other, until at last Robin spied a free table in the corner, and led Brenda through the sea of bobbing, laughing faces towards it. As soon as they sat down, he started to speak, his usually light-hearted manner giving way to one of nervous intensity.

'I owe you a great debt of thanks, I really do.'

'I'm still not sure I did the right thing.' A hole had appeared in the knee of her tights and Brenda, catching sight of it, quickly crossed her legs to hide it.

'I checked what the pills were. If you wanted amphetamines, why not go to your own doctor?'

He stared at her. 'They weren't for *me*.' His voice sounded genuinely injured. 'They were for a friend, my flat mate actually. He's in the same year at med. school as me . . .'

'Your flat mate?' Brenda echoed. 'You mean you took them for someone *else*?'

'I had to,' Robin dropped his eyes in shame. 'I know it's daft saying it now, but . . . I felt I couldn't let him down. He was banking on them.'

'Why couldn't he go to a doctor himself?'

'It's not that simple,' Robin replied. 'He comes from up north, and he hasn't got himself a GP in London. And he couldn't go to the hospital quack.'

'Why not?'

'Because the hospital doctor also happens to be the registrar in the medical team he's attached to. If it got out he was on amphets., it could go against him.'

'Why should it get out?' Brenda asked. 'The doctor wouldn't tell anyone ...'

'He's going to jump to conclusions though isn't he?' replied Robin. 'He's bound to. You don't know what the pressure's like in medical school, Brenda. One exam after another, consultants barking questions at you all the time, and if there's any sign of anyone not being able to keep up with it ...' He shrugged dismissively.

'Since it's your friend who needs them, why didn't he take them himself?'

'He hasn't got access to them on the ward he's attached to.' Robin paused briefly to sip his drink before going on : 'He's re-sitting some exams soon, and he's as anxious as hell about them. Got himself worked into a real lather ... He's had amphets. in the past, and said they helped him, so when I saw that bottle today, I ...' He shrugged again. 'I didn't even think about what I was doing. It was just one of those spur of the moment things, you know ...' He glanced at her. 'I know the risk you took, not telling on me, Brenda. And I want you to know I appreciate it, and it won't happen again. In future he can get his own ruddy pills.' He suddenly smiled, and his whole demeanour changed, the anxious look being replaced by one of boyish charm. 'And I'd like to say I'm sorry I did it, but in a way I'm not. It was worth the risk to bring us together, wasn't it?'

The question threw her for a moment, and she reddened. She had certainly entertained vague hopes that the evening might possibly lead to something, but common sense had warned her not to be too optimistic. He would probably explain about the pills, and they would part. Now it seemed he had other plans, and she found her hopes soaring.

They spent the rest of the evening in the pub. They talked about the hospital, their homes, their hopes for the future. The conversation was fluid and relaxed, and it seemed quite natural, when they eventually left the pub, for Brenda to return to his flat. His flat mate was out, and Robin led Brenda into a small, untidy kitchen where they made instant coffee and discussed films and books. At midnight Robin looked at his watch and said it was time he saw her home, as he had to be up early to trail a consultant's round.

He walked her back to the nurses' home, and they arranged to go to the cinema the following week. Then he kissed her. The kiss, while not particularly passionate, was obviously affectionate, and Brenda responded with enthusiasm. She slept little that night, and when she did she dreamt of Robin and herself sitting at the corner table in the pub. The only disturbing aspect of the dream was that she was drinking, not from a glass, but from a small, brown, pill bottle labelled amphetamines.

The first date was followed by others, and the pattern of their outings invariably followed the same routine. Twice weekly Robin would collect Brenda, either from the ward or the nurses' home, and they would go to the cinema, to a pub or for a meal; if his flat mate was out they would return to his flat and lie entwined on the carpet in front of the gas fire listening to records. At about midnight, or shortly after, Robin would see her home. He had only once tentatively suggested that Brenda stayed the night, but Brenda, a novice in such matters, had made some confused excuse about being on first shift the next day and hastily changed the subject.

Her dates with Robin became increasingly important to her, and she found herself looking forward to them eagerly. But although she was now getting to know Robin better, there were still areas of him which were shrouded in mystery. She had great difficulty in getting him to talk about himself. For the most part he seemed happy to listen to her, and she began to feel vaguely uncomfortable. The snippets of information he gave about himself were so sparse compared with her own long soliloquies. It reminded her of talking to the bespectacled Barbara, where she revealed everything, while the former hid non-committally behind her glasses and revealed nothing. She was also aware that Robin wasn't entirely what he seemed. Although usually relaxed and confident, occasionally he was plunged into a moody silence which disturbed Brenda. It was as though behind that polished exterior there lurked someone very different, a complex, insecure person who was anxious never to reveal himself. There wasn't much Brenda could do, so she pretended to ignore his moods, hoping that as they came to know each other better he would confide in her.

But there was another aspect of their relationship which began to puzzle her. They never met at weekends. Now and again they would meet on a Friday night, but generally their dates fell on mid-weekday evenings. At first Brenda hadn't minded, but as the weeks went by, she found herself longing for him at the weekends, and speculating as to what he got up to in her absence. It occurred to her that he might have another girl friend and the thought upset her. She had once asked him how he spent his weekends and received the vague reply, 'Doing this and that, you know . . .' Most of the other medical students spent their Saturday nights at the many hospital parties, and she started going to them, in the hope that she might meet him there. But his absence was conspicuous. She then tried casually dropping hints about how miserable it was going to parties on your own with all those lecherous medical students around, and he replied, 'Yes, it can't be very nice,' and said no more. Her frustration mounted, and with it her curiosity.

Then one Saturday night things came to a head. She had been going off duty on Friday when Barbara Holmes suddenly caught up with her in the hospital corridor.

'I'm giving a party tomorrow night,' she said, flashing her blue glasses in the general direction of Brenda's face. 'Nothing fancy, just the usual hospital crowd. You're welcome to come if you want to.'

The invitation was as unexpected as it was welcome. As a humble first-year straight from the training school, Brenda had scarcely expected to be included in the social life of a qualified nurse, and she accepted immediately. Barbara hastily scribbled down her address on a scrap of paper, and hurried back to the ward. Brenda decided that this time she would ask Robin to go with her, and that evening she telephoned him.

'Barbara Holmes is giving a party tomorrow night,' she said. 'I wondered if you'd like to come with me?'

She held her breath, waiting for his reply. Finally he said vaguely. 'Tomorrow night? It's a bit difficult actually, Bren. I'm tied up.'

Brenda said nothing.

'I would if I could, love,' he went on in the same vague way. 'But I really can't. I'm sorry.'

'No need to apologise.'

'I'll see you on Tuesday as planned.' If he had noticed the stiffness of her reply, he didn't acknowledge it. 'Same place, same time, all right?'

After they had finished talking Brenda hung up and returned disconsolately to her room. She was angry with him for rejecting her invitation, and angry with herself for showing she cared. She threw herself on to the bed. Well, I'll go alone, she said aloud. That'd show him. But she had the uncomfortable feeling that it wouldn't prove anything, and that he would probably accept her defiant gesture of independence in his usual unperturbed way.

Barbara Holmes' flat was just off Streatham High Road. She shared it with two other nurses, and between them they seemed to have asked the entire hospital to the party. Brenda, looking around the crowded, smoke-filled room, was vainly trying to put names to familiar faces when a tall blonde girl elbowed her way over.

'There you are,' she said, and Brenda realised it was Barbara without her glasses. A small pair of heavily made-up eyes squinted at her short-sightedly. 'There's someone wants to meet you.' She put a hand under Brenda's arm and steered her across the room into the hall. Sitting on the stairs, talking to a thin, angular girl in jeans, was a young man Brenda had never seen before. As they approached him he looked up. He had dark hair, cut unfashionably short, and soft brown eyes which stared quizzically at her.

'This is Brenda,' Barbara said, with the air of a magician producing a rabbit from a hat. 'Brenda, meet Dave Martin,' and apparently satisfied with those brief words of introduction she returned to her guests.

An awkward silence followed, which Dave filled. 'So you're the famous Brenda!' The mouth beneath the brown eyes was smiling, and Brenda smiled slowly back.

'That's right. I'm sorry, I didn't quite catch who you were . . . ?'

'Dave. Dave Martin. I share a flat with Robin.'

Brenda stared at him. Somehow Robin had neglected to tell her his flat mate's name, and the little he had told her about him, didn't fit the figure in front of her. For some reason, possibly because of his connection with the amphetamines, Brenda had always imagined Robin's flat mate to be the intense, long-haired type. This stolid, respectable boy was the opposite. The angular girl in jeans stood up, muttering something about getting a drink, and Dave patted the vacant place on the stair beside him.

'Sit down. I was hoping you'd be here tonight so we

could have a natter.'

Obligingly Brenda sat down. The stairway was narrow and her thigh was crushed against his. She edged nearer the wall.

'I've heard a lot about you,' Dave said. 'In fact I've been telling Robin not to keep you to himself so much. He'll be livid we've finally met. I've somehow had the distinct feeling he's been trying to keep us apart.'

'Really?' Brenda frowned slightly. Now he mentioned it, Robin *had* tended to be rather evasive about Dave. In fact when she had once remarked she'd like to meet him, Robin had said something along the lines that his flat mate was rather shy and didn't like meeting strangers. She looked at Dave. 'Shy' was hardly an adjective she would use. He was grinning at her amiably over a plastic cup of red wine.

'He's a real dark horse old Rob isn't he? Full of contradictions.'

Brenda nodded, and said nothing. It seemed disloyal to discuss Robin in this way, and she wasn't sure she wanted to be party to it. Dave's next remark, however, changed her mind. 'Got himself into a real pickle over these exams hasn't he?'

Brenda gaped at him. 'Exams, what exams?'

'The third year exams. Didn't he tell you? We take them next week. Robin's got himself into his usual state. He failed the last lot and had to re-sit them, and he thinks the same's going to happen again. I've been getting quite worried about him. Not eating, not sleeping, swotting every hour God sends. I'm surprised he finds time to take you out, I really am. He usually cold shoulders girls during these studying stints.'

A nagging doubt started to gnaw at Brenda. 'But I thought it was *you* who got into states over exams.'

David stared at her. 'Me?' He threw back his head and laughed, revealing a row of even, white teeth. 'Good Lord, no! Where did you get that idea? My problem is I can't take any of it seriously enough. I wish I could. Life's too short to spend worrying about exams. Either you pass or you fail, getting all knotted up about it won't help.'

Brenda looked at him searchingly and cleared her throat. 'I know all about it,' she said, dropping her voice to a whisper. 'About the amphetamines I mean. He told me about them.'

Dave's smile faded slightly. 'Amphetamines? What amphetamines?'

'About how you have to take them sometimes.' The doubt in Brenda's mind was growing and she faltered. 'That sometimes you got a bit worked up over exams and . . .' she broke off. Dave was looking at her in bewilderment.

'He told you *I* took amphetamines? Is that what you're saying?'

Brenda nodded, and Dave's cheeks flushed an angry red. 'I don't know what he's been playing at, love, but I'm afraid he's been leading you down the proverbial garden path.'

'You mean you don't take them?'

'Certainly not,' Dave said. 'If anything I disapprove of the damn things, and I've told him so a hundred times.' He paused, frowned and looked at her. 'If you want to know who takes amphetamines, try looking in the cupboard in his room, you'll find your answer.'

The next day was a Sunday, and Brenda spent most of it in bed. She wasn't ill, she simply lacked the energy to get up. Why had Robin lied to her? She could understand him covering up initially, perhaps through shame, but he had had ample opportunity to put her straight at their subsequent meetings. Was that the reason he had been so anxious for her and Dave not to meet, so his secret wouldn't come out? Why had he never told her about these impending exams? What else had he concealed from her? As if seeking sanctuary from her thoughts she burrowed deeper into the bed, and another question suddenly entered her mind. Was that why he had decided to take her out in the first place, to guarantee her silence? Each question was more disturbing than its predecessor, and finally, unable to endure it any longer, she decided to ring him. She got dressed and went downstairs to the phone in the reception area of the nurses' home. But when she heard his voice, her courage failed her, and she hastily hung up. What could she say anyway? He would probably deny it all and say Dave was simply making it all up, to cover himself . . . She plodded back to her room. She would have to talk to him about it when they met on Tuesday, no hysteria, no tantrums, she would simply tell him about her meeting with Dave, and ask if it was true. Yes, that was definitely the way to handle it. And then she could watch his face while she was talking to him, and see if he was telling her the truth.

The following morning she checked in for duty on the ward to find the Ward Sister off sick, and the place in chaos. Three new patients had been admitted during the night and another two were due that morning. On top of that, the consultant was going to do his round that afternoon, and his houseman and a group of medical students were clogging the ward corridor, hastily collating notes on the new patients. Barbara, as acting head of the ward in the Sister's absence, was getting increasingly harassed as the morning wore on. Mrs Meredith, one of the elderly patients, was getting very weak, and the registrar who was handling her case had asked Barbara to ring her husband and inform him of his wife's deteriorating condition. Phone calls like that always distressed Barbara, and this one was no exception. She then discovered that one of the patients who had been admitted during the night was a surgical case, and shouldn't have been in their ward at all. She rang up casualty to try and find out how the mix-up occurred, and they finally tracked down the reason.

Apparently an agency nurse had been on night duty in the ward, and the porter bringing the patients up from casualty was new, and mistook the ward numbers. The agency nurse didn't think to check on the new admission, but had simply put her in a bed, done some routine observations, and thought no more about it. Barbara arranged to have the patient transferred to the surgical ward, and when the porter turned up to collect her, Barbara vented her anger on him, saying that if porters didn't know enough to check ward numbers, they shouldn't be allowed to do the job. The porter, a long-haired young man who went by the name of Pike, listened to her criticisms with a faintly bored air, and then pointed out it wasn't him who'd made the error, and he couldn't be responsible for every half-witted mistake his colleagues made. Brenda, listening to the interchange as she helped an auxiliary manoeuvre the coffee trolley between the houseman and the clump of medical students, felt sorry for Barbara, and when the porter finally ambled off to collect his patient, she asked what she could do to help. Barbara was just finishing giving her an apparently endless list of instructions, when Robin entered the ward corridor.

On seeing him, Brenda immediately reddened, returned his brief nod of salutation with a hasty wave, and gratefully headed off into the ward to obey Barbara's instructions. The first job she had to do was change all the bed linen, but she had only just started when Barbara bustled up.

'Pharmacy has just sent that load of drugs I ordered,' she said, blinking distractedly behind her glasses. 'I'll have to put them in the cupboard, I can't leave them lying in the corridor all morning. You'd better stop that and give me a hand.'

Brenda's heart sank. Going back into the ward corridor meant encountering Robin again, but Barbara was already heading purposefully away, and she had no choice but to follow.

The houseman and medical students were still muttering in the corridor, and she quickly squeezed by and entered the clinical room, where Barbara was unlocking the drugs cupboard. Whenever dangerous drugs came on to the ward, they had to be scrupulously counted, witnessed and signed for, and then entered up in the drugs book. They were then placed into the drugs cupboard, counted once again, and entered into a second book, which recorded the total amount of drugs contained in the cupboard. As they worked, Brenda could hear the houseman and medical students talking behind her, and among the voices was Robin's, incisive and confident, giving out case-history information. Suddenly the voices broke off and another one, pitched high in alarm, could be heard.

'Doctor! Staff!' A second-year student nurse was pushing her way through to the clinical room, her face distorted with panic.

'It's Mrs Meredith, I think she's arrested!'

Barbara scrambled off the stool she was standing on, and headed for the door. 'Get the cardiac arrest unit in here,' she shouted over her shoulder to Brenda. 'On the double!'

Brenda elbowed her way through the jostling medical students in the ward corridor, and nearly collided with Pike, pushing a patient on a trolley. Without stopping to apologise, she dived into the Sister's office and dialled for the cardiac arrest team.

Despite their efforts, Mrs Meredith died. It was hardly a surprise, as this was the second time her heart had stopped, but her death leant an air of gloom to the day. The second-year nurse and Brenda were put in charge of organising her removal from the ward, and they were in the middle of doing it, when an ashen-faced Barbara joined them.

'Nurse Cotteral? I'd like a word please.'

Puzzled by the tone in her voice, Brenda followed her out of the ward into the clinical room. Barbara took off her glasses and rubbed her eyes.

'Some diamorphine is missing.'

Brenda blinked at her. 'Diamorphine?'

'Heroin,' Barbara said impatiently. 'We left the drugs cupboard unlocked when Mrs Meredith arrested. It was my fault, I just upped and left it. Now there's a five ampoule box of diamorphine missing.'

'Are you sure?'

'Of course I'm sure,' Barbara snapped. 'I've checked and double checked. Someone must have lifted them while we were coping with Mrs Meredith. I've phoned through and reported it, but they'll want to see us and . . .' Her voice trailed off. There was a small red mark on the side of her nose where her glasses had been, and she rubbed at it absently. 'They'll want to know exactly who was in the ward corridor and what happened . . .'

Brenda felt a small knot gather in the pit of her stomach. Robin. She tried to dismiss the thought, but it persisted and even blossomed. But why would he take them? Amphetamines were one thing, but diamorphine . . . ? She suddenly felt sick. The unanswered questions about him started to crowd into her mind again. She became aware of Barbara watching her curiously.

'If you know something, Brenda, you'd better tell me.'

'I can't,' Brenda's voice was a hoarse whisper. 'I can't.'

'Look, love, someone's wandering around this hospital with a hundred milligrammes of heroin and we've got to find them before they either use it or sell it.'

The knot in Brenda's stomach tightened. Before she could stop herself she was telling Barbara everything. About the amphetamines, her subsequent dates with Robin, her conversation with Dave . . . She was to repeat it endlessly during the course of the day. To the Senior Nursing Officer, to the hospital's Head of Security, and finally to a baldheaded, cigar-smoking police inspector. She felt as if she were treading on air. As if it were all happening to someone else and she was observing it all from a distance. She was severely reprimanded for not reporting the amphetamine incident, and told to report to the Head of the Nursing School the next day, who would decide what steps to take. Robin was immediately suspended pending an investigation. Brenda made repeated attempts to phone him that evening, but there was no answer.

The following morning, after a sleepless, anxious night, she had her interview with Heather Windrup. Heather showed neither sympathy nor understanding for her actions. She used words like 'disgraceful' and 'irresponsible'. Tearfully Brenda offered her resignation, but instead of accepting it, Heather merely stonily regarded her across her desk. Finally she said she would have to discuss it with the Principal Nursing Officer. In the meantime Brenda was not to return to the ward, but had to remain in the school of nursing and do some theory work until the matter was resolved. Then she dismissed her.

Disconsolately Brenda wandered the corridors. She felt everyone in the hospital knew about the incident, and she kept her head lowered, unable to meet anyone's eyes. Finally she found herself outside the ward. She peered through the porthole windows in the doors, and caught sight of Barbara, who waved to her, and came out.

'Hi,' she said, pushing open the swing doors which separated the ward from the hospital corridor. 'What did Miss Windrup say?'

Brenda told her, and asked if there was any more news about Robin. Barbara shook her head.

'He's still suspended. I got a mouthful from the S.N.O. for leaving the drugs cupboard unlocked. We've had two policemen digging around the ward all morning asking questions, they don't seem to have come up with anything though.' She paused and looked at Brenda curiously from

110

behind her blue lenses. 'Do you really think he did it, Brenda?'

'I don't know,' Brenda tried to keep the tremor out of her voice. 'That's the awful part, I just don't know, and I can't get hold of him to talk to him.'

'You *had* to tell them, love. He must know that. You mustn't blame yourself.'

Brenda, not trusting herself to speak, said nothing. Barbara offered to collect her things from the ward locker room, and disappeared. While Brenda waited, a porter shuffled past her and entered the ward. It was Pike. He glanced at her briefly, and then quickly averted his eyes. Brenda frowned. Something in his furtive manner attracted her attention. She moved to the ward doors. He was ambling up the ward corridor, hands dug into pockets. Then he paused, looked around him, and believing himself to be unobserved, moved over to a small shelf suspended from the wall. On the shelf, anchored by a piece of string, was the dangerous drugs record book. He flicked it open, glanced at it, and closed it, and then continued up the corridor. Brenda bit her lip. Why should a porter be interested in the drugs book? She could feel the knot forming in her stomach again. The only possible reason anyone could be interested in the drugs book was if they wanted to know what drugs were on the ward . . . She moved away from the doors and took a deep breath. Was it possible *Pike* had taken the diamorphine? He had been in the corridor at the time . . . A senior nurse bustled up the corridor and Brenda opened her mouth to speak to her, and then quickly closed it. She had virtually accused one person, she could hardly start accusing another . . . The ward doors suddenly opened again, and Barbara emerged, carrying a pair of shoes and a raincoat.

'Are these yours?' she asked, holding out the shoes.

'No, but the mac is.' Brenda took the raincoat. 'Thanks, Barbara.'

'My pleasure,' Barbara smiled at her and the eyes behind the glasses crinkled. 'I'd better get back, Sister's on. Keep your chin up, eh? All's well that end's well.'

Brenda started up the corridor and then paused. If she were right about Pike, she should tell *someone*, otherwise Robin might never be cleared . . . She was turning around to do just that, when she saw Pike leaving the ward. He was pushing a patient in a wheel chair, and was heading towards the X-ray unit. Instinctively Brenda found herself following him. He delivered the patient to the X-ray and emerged into the corridor again. A moment later, he dodged into another ward, this time male surgical. Brenda watched him from a safe distance. His performance was exactly as it had been previously. A casual amble up the ward corridor, a glance around and then a surreptitious look at the drugs book, followed by a leisurely walk into the ward itself. A few minutes later, she found herself following him down the stairs. She assumed he was going to the porters' lodge on the ground floor to collect more instructions, but instead he continued down the stairs towards the basement.

The basement of the hospital was used mainly by hospital staff. It served as a useful short cut between departments, and also housed various locker rooms used by porters, auxiliaries and cleaners. As Brenda watched, Pike glanced around, and entered one of the locker rooms. He was gone for nearly ten minutes, and Brenda was just beginning to despair when he suddenly re-emerged. He wasn't alone. A squat middle-aged man in a raincoat and battered trilby hat was with him, and after a few moments of heated discussion outside the locker-room door, they separated and headed off in opposite directions down the corridor. Brenda waited until Pike was out of sight, and crossed to the locker-room door. Suppose someone was in there, how could she explain her presence? Quickly she took off her nursing cap and stuffed it in a pocket, and pulled on her civilian mac. If anyone was inside, she would pretend to be a visitor who'd lost her way. She knew it wasn't very convincing, but if she sounded confident enough, it might just work. Cautiously she pushed open the door. The locker room was empty. It was a large, gloomy room, almost completely lined with tall, grey, metal lockers. They reminded Brenda of coffins, and she shuddered at the thought. She looked helplessly about. Which one was Pike's? She moved to one of the lockers. There was nothing on it to reveal its owner. She tugged at the handle. It was locked. Suddenly she heard approaching voices and footsteps, and she frantically looked around for a hiding place. The voices were nearer, louder, the door was opening. On impulse Brenda put her head down and charged out of the room. She caught a glimpse of a startled West Indian face gaping at her, before she ran up the corridor.

Heather Windrup listened impassively while Brenda told her story, then reached for her telephone. Ten minutes later Brenda repeated the whole thing to the police inspector and the Head of Hospital Security. For some reason the man in the trilby hat seemed to interest them more than Pike, and she had to describe him in detail. The police inspector puffed attentively at his cigar, and then asked her to write it all down. When she had finished Heather told her to return to the nurses' home and wait. Back in her room Brenda lay on her bed, and looked at the fine network of cracks on the ceiling. Had they believed her? Suppose she was wrong? Suppose Pike was innocent? But that would make Robin guilty . . . Well, suppose they were *both* innocent? The thoughts spiralled through her head relentlessly and finally, exhausted by the day's traumas, she drifted into an uneasy sleep. She was woken by a knock at the door. Heather entered and sat down on the bed next to her.

'What's happened?' Brenda asked, quickly sitting up.

'Did they believe me?'

Heather nodded. 'That man you saw with Pike, the police know him. He's got a record for pushing drugs. They rushed a warrant through and searched his flat. The diamorphine was there, plus some other drugs Pike had stolen for him. The police are going to charge them both.'

'So Robin's in the clear?'

Heather didn't answer immediately. 'Over the diamorphine he is, certainly. But there's still the question of those amphetamines. The Head of the Medical School hasn't decided what to do about it yet.'

'But he'll be re-instated, surely?'

'I honestly don't know, Brenda.' The use of her Christian name was somehow disconcerting. 'That's not for me to decide. However, what happens to *you*, is my decision. I've discussed it with the powers that be and . . .' she broke off . . . 'I don't mind telling you, when I heard about how you kept silent over those amphetamines I felt like asking for your resignation there and then. But to some extent your actions today have put the record straight. We've decided to forget the whole incident, and I suggest you do the same.'

She looked expectantly at Brenda, waiting for some sign of relief. But all she saw was agitation.

'What about Robin though? Will they really throw him out?'

'We'll know more about that tomorrow. The head of the Medical school is going to tell him his decision then.' Heather looked searchingly at Brenda. 'If it does go against him, Brenda, you mustn't . . .'

'Blame myself?' Brenda bitterly completed the sentence for her.

'You didn't ask to see him taking those pills,' Heather said gently. 'And you proved your loyalty to him by saying nothing at the time. You had to speak out when the diamorphine went missing, you had no choice.'

114

'Try telling him that.'

'Why not tell him yourself?' Heather stood up and automatically smoothed her overall. 'It'll be better coming from the horse's mouth, won't it?'

Brenda went round to Robin's flat that evening. At first, when she rang the bell, it seemed no one was in, and relief flooded over her. Then the door abruptly opened a crack, and Robin's face appeared. He looked at her silently for a moment, and then opened the door wider so that she could enter. They passed Dave on the landing, on his way out. Robin paused on the stairs, and said pointedly: 'Of course, you two have already met, haven't you? So introductions aren't necessary.' Dave gave Brenda a short, embarrassed nod, and continued on down.

The sitting-room was a jumble of suitcases and books. Brenda looked around at them as she entered, and then looked at Robin.

'You're going away.' It was a statement rather than a question.

He nodded and picked up a book. It was a medical dictionary. He leafed through it absently as he spoke.

'I've decided to resign. I've just written a note to the Head of the Med. School, Dave's delivering it now.'

'*Why*? You might have been re-instated . . .'

'Not a chance. And even if I was . . .' He broke off, looked at the book in his hands, and abruptly tossed it on to the sofa. 'I don't want to go on with it anyway. It was all getting too much, the pressure and . . . That's how all this started, because I couldn't keep up.' He turned to face her. 'I'm no good at it, if you want the truth.' She was about to interrupt, but he waved her to silence. 'I went into medicine because it had always been a childhood ambition. But it's been uphill work from the word go. Even in the first year I was lagging behind . . . It's all right for someone like Dave, he can take it in his stride. Me, I just can't seem to cope with it. That's why I took the amphets., to keep myself going while I studied. But I was slipping behind, I know I was.'

'You always seemed so . . .' Brenda paused, searching for the right word. He found it for her.

'Confident? That's all part of the act. If they knew how I really felt . . . I wouldn't have had a dog's chance! But the exams always told the truth. I only just scraped through the re-sits of the last ones . . . I'm just not cut out for it, it's as simple as that.'

Brenda stared at him. So this was the other side of him she had always wondered about. Aloud she said, 'Where will you go, what will you do?'

He shrugged. 'Art school perhaps. I don't know. That's what I wanted to do once, but I thought medicine was more secure . . .' He looked at her gravely. 'I would have told you about it, but – ' he paused – 'it seemed simpler to say it was Dave who needed the amphets. and keep quiet. I wasn't sure how you'd take it, if you thought they were for me.'

'Did you really care how I'd take it, Robin?'

He looked at her, puzzled. 'Of course I did. I cared very much. Why else would I have taken you out? I would have taken you out more if it hadn't been for those exams hanging over me . . . As it was I had to spend every weekend studying.' His words washed over her. So *that* was how he'd spent his weekends. She lowered herself into an armchair.

'And having said they were for Dave,' he went on, 'I couldn't spoil the story by telling you about my exam worries, could I? So I carried on with the pretence. Then that diamorphine went missing and you blew the whistle on me . . . In a way, I'm glad you did. At least it put an end to the charade, something I never had the courage to do.'

Brenda looked down at her hands, limply lying in her lap. 'I've ruined your career.'

'Melodrama doesn't suit you, Bren.,' he said. 'That's one

of the things I always liked about you. No fuss, no frills. No, my career was already threatened, you just brought it to a head that's all. Although . . .' His voice trailed off, and Brenda looked up at him.

'Although what?'

He looked at her with a small frown. 'I've been wondering, did you really think that I stole that diamorphine?'

Haltingly Brenda tried to explain to him about her confused feelings after her meeting with Dave. 'I didn't know what to think,' she finished lamely. 'So many things didn't fit. And I was upset you hadn't told me the truth from the start.'

'So blowing the whistle on me was your revenge?'

'No!' Brenda said vehemently, and then frowned. 'No . . . I . . . I felt I had to tell them. In case . . .' She broke off. A moment of awkward silence followed. Robin moved back to his suitcases and books.

'What happens now?' Brenda asked

'I told you. I'm going away. Try and sort out what it is I really want to do.'

'I meant . . .' Brenda hesitated, 'I meant with us.'

He looked at her across ·the room. 'What would you suggest?'

'Now we've got everything out into the open . . .' Brenda shrugged helplessly. 'I'd like to carry on.'

'Pretend none of this ever happened?'

'Why not?'

Robin stood up. 'I think a relationship needs to be based on more than a pretence,' he said gently. 'That's where we went wrong before. If it's going to work, it needs trust. And that's something neither of us seems to be very good at, is it?'

Brenda looked down at her unfinished letter. Was there really any point in telling her parents all about it? Robin was now thousands of miles away in Canada, apparently staying with his brother. Had *he* felt the need to tell anyone about it? She doubted it somehow. Anyway, perhaps it was better left untold. Perhaps it was better to do as Miss Windrup suggested, and forget the whole thing. She tore up the letter with its pages of closely spaced writing, and dropped it in the waste bin. Then she picked up her pen again, considered a moment, and started writing . . .

'Dear Mummy and Daddy,

Thank you for your letters. I'm sorry I haven't written back for so long, but I've been very busy. Everything is fine here, and I've no real news. How are things in Devon? . . . . . .

Nights

'Ovaltine, Bournvita, hot chocolate, Horlicks, cocoa . . .'

The S.E.N. nurse pulled the hot drinks trolley to a halt beside Roy's bed. 'Name your poison then.'

Roy slowly turned his head to look at her. Even that slight movement was difficult for him. One of his legs was encased in plaster, and his pelvis was supported by a sling, hung on a frame above the bed. One arm was also in plaster. He was in his early twenties, and in hospital as a result of a motor cycle accident. He blinked at her laconically, from under heavy-lidded eyes.

'How long have I been in here, darling?'

' "Nurse", if you don't mind.'

Roy ignored the correction. 'Going on two months, right? And I always have the same drink. Always chocolate. Yet you still have to go through that routine, every flaming night.

The S.E.N. smiled, unperturbed. She was used to Roy's type and regarded them as a daily hazard of the job. She reached for a jug on the trolley. 'Chocolate it is then.'

'Hooray.'

Still smiling, the S.E.N. poured the chocolate and placed the cup on his bed table. 'Get out of bed the wrong side did we?'

Roy's lips parted in a sneer. 'Ha ha.'

Her smile broadened. 'I put extra sugar in, sweeten you up a bit. Take a whole packet, that, though, and sugar's pricey these days.'

Roy turned away. 'I'll die laughing.'

'That's me love, a barrel of laughs,' she pushed the trolley on a few feet and addressed the inmate of the neighbouring bed.

'Ovaltine, Bournvita, hot chocolate, Horlicks, cocoa . . .?'

'Cocoa please.' The patient was Tom Whittaker. He was a gently-spoken nineteen-year-old, and unlike most of the patients in the orthopaedic ward, he wasn't in traction. On the locker by his bed was a pile of engineering text-books, not the time-killing fiction most patients preferred.

'One cocoa coming up.' The S.E.N. slopped the dark liquid into a cup. 'With or without sugar?'

'Without please.'

Roy turned to look curiously at his neighbour. The politeness of Tom's tone irritated him. In fact everything about Tom irritated him, perhaps because they were such opposites. Roy had a natural, instinctive kind of intelligence, but lack of education or indolence, or a combination of both, had prevented him from using it in any kind of useful way. As a result he was restless and bored. His boredom showed itself in the constant needling of those around him. And Tom happened to be near him, and so had to suffer for it.

'You're sweet enough already, right, Tom?'

Tom made no reply, and the S.E.N. glanced reprovingly at Roy. 'That's enough of that, Roy.'

Roy was still looking at Tom. 'Oy, Tom. I'm talking to you.'

Tom said nothing and the S.E.N. moved towards him, bearing his cup of cocoa. 'Ignore him, love,' she said in a low, almost conspiratorial tone. 'He's only trying to get a rise out of you, don't give him the satisfaction.' She patted his bed absently, and returned to the trolley and her round. Tom watched her weave her way up the ward, and raised his cocoa cup to his lips. As he did, Roy spoke again.

'Know what they put in this stuff, Tom? The nurses?'

Tom glanced at him, and shook his head.

'Bromide,' Roy grinned, revealing a row of chipped teeth. 'Like in the army. Stops you getting randy.' His smile faded as he looked at Tom's delicate features and his slim body lying under the bedclothes. 'Not much danger of that though is there? Not in your case.'

Tom flushed and put his cocoa on his bedside table, picking up one of the technical books. Turning his back pointedly to Roy, he opened his book and started to read.

Nurses either tend to like, or hate, night duty, and Katey hated it. The truth was it frightened her. She felt that somehow situations at night always seemed magnified, and problems that much bigger. She knew that it was absurd to feel this way, after nearly three years' training, but as she signed in for night duty on the orthopaedic ward, all her old anxieties and doubts came flooding back. She had once tried to analyse why she so disliked night duty, and decided it must be because of the isolation. During the day, if a patient suddenly relapsed, it was simply a question of calling the Ward Sister. But at night there was no Ward Sister on duty. True, she could always telephone for a doctor or a senior nursing officer, but if her assessment of the patient's condition proved incorrect or exaggerated, it could make her very unpopular. Doctors do not like being dragged unnecessarily from their beds, and the night Sisters had enough to do without coping with calls from panicky students. One of the reasons Katey tended to panic on night duty was because she felt she didn't know enough theory. As far as the practical, bedside aspect of nursing went, she was second to none, but she was less confident about the theoretical side. S.R.N. nurses are expected to understand the fundamental medical principles behind the diagnosis, treatment and cure of patients suffering from the more common conditions, and they learn this in lectures. Katey was no academic, and she knew it. She had once confided this to Heather Windrup during a progress interview in her second year, but Heather reassured her by saying that the sign of a good nurse was how she actually handled her patients, not knowing the medical dictionary by heart. However the prospect of being in charge of nearly thirty patients at night, still daunted her, and she found herself telling Jay Harper of her fears, as she scrambled into her uniform in the ward locker room.

'It's all in the mind,' Jay said, buttoning her coat, and glancing at the window. 'Just look at that rain, I'm going to get soaked.'

'Don't *you* ever feel it though?' Katey asked. 'When you do night duty?'

'Feel what?'

'Well . . . anxious.'

'Not really. I quite like it actually . . . There's no one to boss you around.' Jay glanced at Katey's pensive face. 'Anyway, I thought they were going to send an agency nurse to help you?'

Katey brightened. 'Are they? I imagined I was going to be on with a junior.'

Jay shook her head. 'I'm sure I heard Sister ordering one before she went off duty. A Nurse Tate I think she's called . . . So your problem's solved isn't it?' She reached for an umbrella. 'Mind you, I'm not sure how much use these agency nurses are myself, I mean they don't know the ward or the patients or . . .'

'At least she'll be qualified,' Katey said earnestly. 'So if anything happens she can carry the can.'

Jay looked at her curiously. 'That doesn't sound like you, Katey, ducking responsibility . . .'

'I told you, it's just night duty.' Katey gave her a weak smile. 'It plays havoc with me confidence.'

Jay smiled back, and headed for the door. 'I don't know why it should, a good nurse is a good nurse whatever shift she's on.' She suddenly frowned, and paused. 'Oh, and before I forget. Nil by mouth for Tom Whittaker after midnight, he's due for his op. tomorrow.'

'Tom Whittaker,' Katey scratched a quick note on the inside corner of her apron. 'Which bed?'

'Number four. Next to Roy Tucker, the one in the pelvic sling.' She chewed her lip thoughtfully. 'You'd better keep an eye on him, while you're at it . . . he's starting to play up.

The consultant saw him today and Roy was hoping to hear he'd be discharged soon. Apparently he's got to stay in another three months. He's really browned off about it.'

'Right, I'll watch him. Anything else?'

'Nope, that's it.' Jay glanced at the window, 'Just my luck, I'm supposed to be going to a late night barbecue tonight, I suppose it'll be rained off now.' She opened the door. 'I'll see you in the morning. Hope you have a quiet night.'

'Me too,' Katey replied with feeling, but the door was already closing and a moment later she could hear Jay's feet rapidly retreating up the ward corridor. Katey sighed. That was another thing about night duty she didn't like. Being stuck in a ward of sleeping patients, while your friends are all out enjoying themselves. She heard the distant sound of a telephone ringing and roused herself. Well, who knows, she thought as she opened the door, maybe it will be a quiet night, and then you'll have nothing to worry about will you?

The telephone that Katey heard ringing was in the Nursing Administration office. The door suddenly swung open and a figure pounced on the ringing phone. Just as she reached it however, it suddenly hiccuped and stopped.

'Damn.' Myra Tripp banged the phone back on to the receiver and started to unbutton her macintosh. She was a tall, angular woman in her early thirties with a shock of angry red hair. Then the telephone rang again.

'Nursing Administration?' She frowned, as she heard there was a Nurse Tate to speak to her, from the agency. 'O.K., put her through.' After a series of clicks, she heard Carol Tate's voice, and groaned inwardly as she recognised it. She had run up against this particular nurse before. She was notorious for unpunctuality and absenteeism. She listened wearily as Nurse Tate told her she would be unable to come on duty that night as she had suddenly developed flu and a terrible cough.

'You can hear for yourself how bad it is,' Nurse Tate gasped, giving her a quick demonstration of a chest-racking cough. 'I can't come on duty with a cough like that, can I?'

'I suppose not,' Myra said, pulling out a chair and sitting down. 'It came on rather suddenly though didn't it, this cough? I mean, you were only booked this afternoon and you presumably thought you were all right for duty then?'

Nurse Tate agreed, and immediately flung herself into a long explanation how weak chests ran in her family. Myra cut her short.

'I don't want to give the impression that the hospital would exactly collapse without you, Nurse Tate, but your presence does have a certain value, if only to swell the ranks.' Nurse Tate attempted to say something, but she ploughed on quickly : 'I'm not accusing you of anything, my love. In fact I'm full of sympathy. Anyone that can get flu, not to mention coughs, as many times as you, deserves all the sympathy she can get.' She paused to let that one sink in, and then continued : 'I'll just have to try and get a replacement from the hospital pool I suppose, but it won't be easy. In the meantime, Nurse Tate, do me a small favour will you?' She smiled grimly down the mouthpiece. 'Next time you feel flu or a cough coming, give us a little more warning, eh? I would appreciate it!' And before Nurse Tate could make any further proclamations of innocence, she hung up.

'Nurse Tate?'

Katey frowned, bewildered at the S.E.N.'s reaction. 'That's what Jay said she was called. What's so funny?'

The S.E.N. giggled. As they talked, they dragged the desk into the centre of the ward, plugged in the anglepoise lamp, put out charts, pens and a torch, ready for the night ahead.

'She always wriggles out of night duty, that one,' the

S.E.N. said. 'It's a well-known fact.'

Katey gazed at her in consternation. 'I can't manage on my own.'

The S.E.N. shrugged. 'You might have to. Ten to one she won't turn up.' She grinned. 'She reckons her bloke'll get up to mischief if she lets him out of her sight, which he would of course.' She caught sight of a patient stirring out of the corner of her eye, and shouted across to him : 'Try and lie still, eh, Mr Lyle? You'll lose all your bedclothes that way !'

'It's not fair . . .' Katey said plaintively. 'If the Ward Sister booked her, then she should turn up.'

'It's no good moaning to me, love. I'm about to go off duty in a minute.' The S.E.N. stood back to admire her handiwork with the desk, and then glanced at the ward doors where Myra was entering with the drugs trolley. 'Tell Miss Tripp if you're that worried about it.'

Katey frowned, and after a brief moment of hesitation, walked up the ward towards Myra Tripp.

'Evening, Nurse Betts,' Myra said. 'I'm just going to do the drugs round, if you'd like to help me.'

'Yes, Miss Tripp.' Katey cautiously cleared her throat. 'I . . . I understand there's supposed to be an agency nurse on with me tonight? A Nurse Tate?'

'That's right.' Myra briskly unlocked the drugs trolley and critically surveyed the jumble of bottles and jars inside it. 'Usual mess. Typical of the day staff to leave it for us to sort out.'

Katey took a step towards her and lowered her voice. 'The thing is, Miss Tripp, she doesn't seem to have turned up.'

'Eh?'

'The agency nurse. She hasn't turned up yet.'

'She won't either,' Myra replied. 'She rang in to say she's got flu.'

'But I can't manage on my own . . .' It was out before

126

Katey could stop it, and Myra looked at her sharply.

'I hope you haven't got one of these night-duty phobias. Why is it perfectly capable girls often go to pieces at the idea of being on the ward at night? Something I've never been able to understand.'

Katey blushed slightly. 'I just prefer to have someone on with me . . .'

'Well, it so happens you're in luck,' Myra said. 'I've ordered a relief nurse from the hospital pool. Should be along at any minute.'

Katey breathed a small sigh of relief. 'Fantastic! Thanks, Miss Tripp.'

Myra glanced at her shrewdly. 'Although why someone as competent as you should be so worried, I really can't imagine . . .'

The S.E.N. nurse interrupted them. 'I'm off now, Miss Tripp, if that's O.K.?'

Myra smiled. 'I dare say we'll manage without you, love,' she said with a smile. 'See you in the morning.'

'Righto.' The S.E.N. moved towards the ward doors and waved airily at Katey as she passed. 'Have a good night. Don't do anything I wouldn't do.'

Myra turned back to Katey. 'Well, let's get on shall we?' She picked up a pill bottle, checked it against a clipboard of papers, and addressed a patient. 'Now then, Mr Naylor, what can we tempt you with tonight?'

On the other side of the ward, Roy Tucker watched the drugs trolley manoeuvering round the beds with ill-concealed impatience. He had long since discovered that the only relief to his boredom was to retreat into the relaxing cloak of unconsciousness provided by his nightly sleeping pill. A slight movement from Tom caused him to glance over. Tom was lying on his side, with his back to Roy. A small smile strayed round Roy's lips. Holding on to the handle dangling from the frame above his bed, he pulled himself up slightly, and addressed the turned back.

'Tom?'

The back shifted imperceptibly, but made no response.

'Not worried about it are you, Tom? Your op. tomorrow?'

Still no response. Roy sank back against his pillows.

'Ever been behind a butcher's shop, Tom? Seen all the carcasses laid out on the slabs?' He looked pointedly at Tom's back. 'That's where they carve them up. They've got these meat cleavers . . . huge things . . . and sharp . . .' He whistled softly, through his chipped teeth. 'Cut through anything. Not a pretty sight, Tom, I can tell you. Not a sight for the squeamish.' He dropped his voice to a whisper. 'Still, not so bad when it isn't your own. You can think of it like ink can't you? Red ink. When it's your own though . . .' he paused meaningfully . . . 'well, that's altogether different. Know what I mean, Tom? Eh?'

Unseen by him, Tom stirred and put a hand over his eyes, as if trying to shut out the image that Roy's words had evoked. He was spared from making a reply by Myra's intervention.

'Hello, Sunshine.' Myra pulled the trolley to a halt by Roy's bed. 'And how are you tonight?'

'How do I look?'

Myra grinned. 'Miserable, since you ask.'

'Well then.'

Myra consulted her clipboard. 'You want a sleeping pill?'

'Why not.'

Myra nodded to Katey, who shook a red and yellow capsule into a small plastic cup, before turning back to Roy.

'You're still on tranquillisers aren't you?'

Roy nodded. 'You know me, love. Whatever's going, I'll have.'

Myra looked at him thoughtfully, registering his downward tone. 'Cheer up, Roy. They'll have that plaster off before long, you wait and see.'

'Fat chance.' Roy hoisted himself on his elbow to look at her. 'The doc. was round today, so I asked him straight out. I looked him in the eye and popped the question.'

'What did he say?'

'He didn't. He shuffled about a bit. Cleared his throat a few times. Muttered on about fractured femurs and how long they take to heal . . . I kept on at him though. Kept on until he told me.'

'And?'

'Another three months. That's what he said. *At least* another three months.'

Myra frowned sympathetically. 'That's bad luck.'

'Three flaming months.' Roy leaned over and picked up a scrap of paper from his bed table. 'I worked it out. Three months, or thirteen weeks, split into days, is ninety-one. Split ninety-one days into hours, and you've got one thousand, one hundred and eighty-four.' As he talked, Myra and Katey exchanged a glance. 'Multiply *that* by sixty, and you've got one hundred and thirty-one thousand and forty minutes.' He looked triumphantly at Myra. 'Which makes a grand total of eight million seconds. Give or take a couple of hundred thousand.'

A moment of awkward silence followed which Myra filled. 'You have been busy.'

Roy tossed the scrap of paper dismissively on to his bed table. 'Beats making raffia mats, doesn't it?'

Myra passed him the plastic cup containing the sleeping pill. 'And what about visitors. Have you had any lately?'

Roy shook his head. 'Have I, hell! Couldn't keep 'em away at first. Had to bring up extra chairs even. Didn't last though. Like the chat. They ran out of things to say, so they stopped coming.'

Myra smiled, trying to lighten his mood. 'Never mind, we still love you.' She poured out a glass of water and handed

E

it to him. 'Now, take that pill and try and get a good night's sleep, eh? You'll feel all the better for it.'

Roy looked pointedly at the pill, and then up at her. 'You reckon, do you?'

'Just hang on in there a bit longer, eh, Roy? You've been terrific up to now.'

'Model patient?'

'The best.'

'Yeah, well. All good things come to an end, as they say.' He looked over at Tom in the neighbouring bed. 'Isn't that right, Tom?'

Myra followed his glance and frowned. Something in Roy's ominous tone alerted a warning bell in her head. She pushed the trolley towards Tom.

'I don't seem to know this one,' she whispered to Katey. 'Is he new?'

'Admitted yesterday,' Katey whispered back. 'By appointment. He's being operated on tomorrow afternoon.'

'Get the notes will you, love? They're probably still in Sister's office. I'd like some background info.'

Katey nodded, and headed out of the ward. While waiting for the notes, Myra tried to engage Tom in conversation.

'What does the "T" stand for?'

'Pardon?'

'Your Christian name?' Myra tapped the name tag on the foot of his bed.

'Tom. Thomas.'

'Welcome to the madhouse, Tom. Settling in all right?'

He gave a small nod by way of reply. Myra beamed encouragingly.

'You'll get used to us. Always takes a day or two . . .' She reached into the drugs trolley and picked up a bottle of tablets. 'Let's see what these do for you, shall we?'

Tom looked at them suspiciously. 'What are they?'

'Just sleeping pills.' He frowned slightly. 'It's all right.

130

They won't poison you.'

Tom ran his tongue over his lips. 'I'd rather not, actually.'

'Doctor's orders, I'm afraid.'

'I'm sorry,' a stubborn thread had entered his voice. 'But I don't – ' he broke off, as if searching for the right words – 'I don't use them,' he said finally, and then added politely, 'Thank you just the same.'

Myra looked at him curiously. 'Why not try one, to get you off to sleep? Big day tomorrow after all, you'll need all the sleep you can get.'

He shook his head. 'No. I'm sorry, but . . . no.'

Myra was opening her mouth to attempt further persuasion when Katey intervened.

'Excuse me, Miss Tripp,' Myra turned to her. 'They've sent a male one.'

Myra looked at her blankly.

'The replacement for Nurse Tate.' Katey glanced around and lowered her voice : 'They've sent a male nurse.'

'What about it?'

'Well I . . .' Katey paused. Like many of her colleagues she was disconcerted by male nurses. It seemed, to Katey's way of thinking anyway, an odd profession for a man to want to enter. She had once voiced this opinion to Jay Harper, who had accused her of chauvinism.

But the prospect of spending an entire night duty with a male nurse daunted her immeasurably.

'I don't feel . . . comfortable with them,' she said lamely. 'It's silly I know, but . . .'

'Very silly,' Myra cut in sharply. 'And time you got over it. Where is he?'

'In the office.'

However the office, when Myra eventually came to look in it, was empty, and eventually she tracked the nurse down in the kitchen, pouring himself a cup of coffee.

'Miss Tripp,' she said, extending a hand. 'Two pee's.

And you are . . . ?'

'Larry Parker.'

Larry Parker was in his mid twenties. He was nearly six foot, with long dark hair which curled over his collar. His beard, masking most of his face, was lighter in colour, and the effect was somehow strange. As if the beard didn't match its owner. Still, he seemed confident enough, which was the main thing if he was to be left in charge.

'Are you familiar with this ward?'

'More or less.'

'Right. Let's get on.' She led the way out of the kitchen into the office. 'You're on with a third year, Katey Betts, you know her?'

The forest on his chin parted into a smile. 'We met. Just a minute ago.'

'She's a bit lacking in confidence about night duty for some reason, but she'll do.' Myra passed him the drugs keys. 'Drugs round's done. Hourly rubs needed for Dunkley and Blake, it's all in the book. If you need me, just bleep.'

Larry gave her a lop-sided grin. 'I might just take you up on that.'

Myra frowned slightly. That warning bell in her head was ringing again. He almost seemed *too* confident, this one. She shrugged the thought away and headed for the door.

'I'll leave you to it, then. I'll be in later, see how you're getting on. And any problems, remember just . . .'

Larry's lips parted in another smile : 'Bleep you. I'll bear it in mind.'

A few minutes later he entered the ward. Most of the patients were now settling in to sleep, and the ward was in semi-darkness. Larry moved to the drugs trolley, checked it was locked, and then sauntered up the ward, pausing at the foot of each bed to check a chart or a patient's name. He reminded Katey, watching him from the desk, of a soldier checking his platoon. He almost seemed to enjoy the sense of power it gave him. As he passed her, he nodded briefly, his lips curling into a grin.

'We meet again.'

Katey smiled limply in reply, and watched him continue his slow passage round the darkened ward. Finally he reached the last bed, pivoted round on his heel, and walked back to the desk. He pulled out the chair next to Katey and sat down. Katey immersed herself in her text-book. The ward suddenly fell quiet, the silence only broken by the occasional discreet cough from a patient, and the rain, spattering on the windows. The figure in the chair next to her stirred slightly, and spoke.

'Drugs chart.'

Katey looked up from her book. 'Pardon?'

'I'd like a dekko at the drugs chart. If you've got it handy?' Katey passed him the clipboard containing the record of drugs administered to the patients. He flipped the papers over, frowned, then glanced at her.

'Which one is Whittaker?'

Katey pointed to Tom's bed. Larry looked down at the clipboard.

'I see he didn't take his sleeping pills.'

'He didn't want them.'

'Or his sedatives?'

'He didn't want those either, apparently.'

'Why's that?'

Katey shrugged. 'He didn't say.'

'Did you ask him?'

Katey paused before replying. What was this anyway – an interrogation? Aloud she said, 'Miss Tripp dealt with it.'

'Ah.' Larry put the clipboard down and looked over towards Tom's bed. 'He's in for a long night then, isn't he?'

Roy was lying on his back, with his head turned to one side, looking at the clock above the ward doors. It was his favourite occupation. Each time the minute hand moved on, he felt it was one less minute to spend imprisoned in the confines of his plaster and the hospital. A sigh from the next bed punctured his thoughts. He swung his head round to look at his neighbour.

'Can't you sleep, Tom?' He dropped his voice to a melodramatic whisper. 'Afraid to, is that it, eh? Afraid of the dreams you'll have about your op.? Is that it, eh, Tom?'

Tom didn't answer, and Roy smiled slightly. Well, it'll give him something to think about, he thought, and turned his eyes back to the clock. The minute hand had clicked on one digit.

'You're from the pool then?'

They had sat in awkward silence for some minutes, and Katey felt she should take the initiative to break it. Larry nodded.

'I was on casualty when they rang.' He shot her a sideways glance. 'You done casualty yet?'

'Last year. I spent six weeks there.'

'It's a joke isn't it?' The question didn't seem to demand an answer and he didn't wait for one. 'We admitted this bloke about eight o'clock, a real tough nut type. Knife wound in his thigh. Then a few minutes later we admitted another one. Fourteen stitches in his neck. Turns out they were fighting each other. Now they're in next door beds, happy as sandboys, comparing scars.' His voice hardened fractionally. 'Senseless.'

Katey gave a small shrug. 'It's London isn't it?'

'Eh?'

'Violence. It goes with city life.'

'It goes with human nature, love.' A movement at the end of the ward caught his attention. 'Hello . . . ?'

Katey turned to see Tom Whittaker getting out of bed and reaching for a dressing-gown. She started to rise from

134

the table, when Larry placed a restraining hand on her arm.

'It's o.k. I'll see to him.'

Once inside the ward corridor, Tom paused to glance around, looking for the kitchen. At the far end of the corridor he saw an open door, and beyond it he could just make out the vague outline of a table and a sink. Slowly he limped towards it. Larry, entering the corridor from the ward, pulled up and watched Tom's slow progress to the kitchen. The limp was fairly pronounced, as if one leg was slightly shorter than the other, giving him a rolling, almost lop-sided gait.

Larry waited until Tom entered the kitchen, and then quietly made his way up the corridor. He stood by the open door and watched, as Tom took a glass from a shelf and filled it with tap water. He had just raised it to his lips, when Larry spoke. 'Can't sleep, eh, Squire?'

Tom lowered the glass and turned to look at him. His shallow blue eyes had a disconcerting intensity of feeling in them.

'I'll be all right.' He gulped back some of the water and carefully placed the half empty glass on the draining board. 'I was a bity thirsty, that's all.'

'Ah.' Larry didn't mention the fact that Tom had a water jug on his bed table.

Tom studied him for a second. 'Are you a nurse?'

'That's the general idea.'

Tom nodded, as if this was the answer he both expected and wanted.

'Well, I'd like to change beds, please.'

'Change . . . ?'

'If it's possible,' Tom said politely, 'I'd like a different bed.'

'It's late. Have a word with the day staff, eh?'

'There is an empty one. Further up the ward, I've seen it.'

'No can do, mate,' Larry replied. 'Means changing the

linen. We'll disturb the other patients.'

'Oh.' There was a wealth of feeling in the one word, and Larry frowned curiously.

'What's the matter with the one you're in?'

Tom hesitated, as if weighing up whether or not to speak. He seemed to decide against it, and gave a mute shrug by way of reply.

Larry moved into the room and perched on the edge of the table. 'You didn't take your sleeping pills.'

'No.'

'Why was that?'

'I don't . . . use them.' Tom paused and then added carefully : 'Not any more.'

'Allergic, eh?'

'No . . .'

Larry shot him a puzzled glance. 'Why then?'

'I just prefer not to take them, that's all.'

Larry shrugged. 'Suit yourself.' He reached into a pocket and withdrew the drugs keys. 'I'll get you a tranquilliser. Soon settle you down.'

'No!' Tom spoke unintentionally sharply, and Larry looked at him in surprise.

'It'll help you relax . . .'

'I'll do my breathing exercises.' Tom pulled his dressing-gown cord around him and started towards the door. 'I prefer to do that, than to take drugs. Prefer to rely on myself.'

'Breathing exercises?'

'Shallow breathing.' Tom reddened slightly. 'Pregnant women do it, to help them relax.'

Larry grinned. 'Do they now. And does it work?'

'Sometimes. If I concentrate.' Tom moved into the open doorway. 'I'll be all right now. Thank you.'

'What are you in for?'

Almost reluctantly Tom turned back. 'I'm having my leg

reset,' he said. He had a precise, considered way of speaking, as if every word had been thought out beforehand. 'It broke and it never set properly. They're going to reset it for me.'

'When did you break it?'

'Seven years ago.'

Larry raised his eyebrows. 'You waited a long time.'

Tom said nothing, merely gave a small nod of agreement. Larry switched off the kitchen light and they moved into the corridor.

'Well, they're first rate here, the ortho. surgeons. You couldn't ask for better ones.'

Tom shot him a swift look, and quickly averted his eyes. 'He said . . . the surgeon who's doing it . . . he said they'd have to break the bone.'

'It's not as bad as it sounds,' Larry said easily. 'They have to break it in order to reset it. Nothing to worry about.' He paused, glancing shrewdly at Tom. 'You aren't worried about it, are you?'

Tom didn't reply for a moment, then he said, 'I'll try and get some sleep now I think.' And before Larry could speak, he shuffled quickly up the corridor into the ward.

A few minutes later Larry rejoined Katey.

'Anything wrong?'

'He's all tensed up,' Larry replied.

'About his op.?'

'About something, that's for sure. Fancy a coffee?'

Katey glanced doubtfully at the sleeping patients surrounding them. 'Should we leave the ward?'

Larry looked around and shrugged. 'Most of them are out for the count. They won't miss us.'

'All the same . . .'

'Come on . . .' A slightly impatient note entered his voice. 'What's five minutes here or there? We've got the half-hourly rubs coming up. Then we'll miss our chance.'

'If you think it's all right.' Katey picked up the torch.

'You're in charge.'

'I'll put the kettle on.' Larry padded out, and Katey slowly followed, flashing her torch over the patients as she went.

Roy quickly closed his eyes as the beam from the torch travelled over him, and waited for the ward doors to swing closed behind Katey, before he opened his eyes and turned to look at Tom.

'Tom? Eh, Tom?'

If Tom had heard him, he had apparently decided not to register it. Roy sighed and looked at the clock.

'Eleven o'clock on a Friday night. Don't suppose Fridays mean much to you, eh, Tom? Being a college boy.' He propped himself on an elbow and looked at the figure in the bed next to him. 'You *are* a college boy, aren't you?'

'University,' Tom replied wearily, realising that Roy would persist until he got an answer. 'If you really want to know, I'm at university.'

'Well, when you work all week,' Roy went on, ignoring Tom's comment, 'I mean *really* work, Friday nights, Saturday nights, you live for them. Count the days, the minutes even . . .' He looked back at the clock over the door. 'We had this clock in the shop, like that one. It didn't have a second hand either. It gave the same click, as it moved on. And each time I'd think, one down, fifty nine to go.' He paused. 'Click.' His thin face mellowed slightly. 'Know what I used to do of a Friday night, Tom? After I got shot of that butcher's shop, after I'd changed, I'd go down the club for a bit, then I'd be away . . .' He smiled at the memory. 'Ever ridden a motor bike, Tom? I had a beauty. A gem. A thousand cc. Four cylinder, water cooled engine, overhead cam., electric start . . .' His face suddenly clouded. 'Came off it on a bend. Took it too wide. Hit that barrier like a cannon ball . . . No time to feel fear. No time to feel anything. Just that barrier, coming out of the dark towards me.' He shut his eyes briefly, as if trying to erase the image, and then opened them and looked at the clock. 'Two down, fifty-eight to go. Click.'

'You'd better turn it off, or you'll flatten it.'

Katey, seated at the kitchen table, glanced down at the torch in her hands, and snapped it off. Larry spooned some coffee into two mugs, and shot her a quick glance.

'Something on your mind?'

'I just don't care for nights.'

'Since when?'

'Since always. I've never cared for them.'

'And does that go for male nurses as well?'

Katey looked at him in surprise. 'What makes you think that?'

He grinned. 'Your face when I arrived. You didn't exactly look bowled over to see me!'

Katey reddened, and his grin broadened. 'It's all right. You're not alone. And they call it a man's world! Not in nursing it's not.'

'Why come into it then?'

'Ah. The sixty-four thousand dollar question.' He pulled out a stool and sat opposite her. 'Why did you?'

'Lots of reasons I suppose.'

'Such as?'

Katey thought a moment before replying. 'Well, I like helping people, seeing them get better, knowing that I am part of it, part of a team . . . And I knew it was the one thing I was really good at. That I might achieve something in.'

'Maybe it was the same with me.'

She looked at him curiously. 'Was it?'

'Could have been.'

Katey frowned. 'It seems such an odd thing, for a man to want to do, I mean . . .'

Larry's lips parted in a smile. 'Men become doctors. Is

the motive so different?'

'Why not be a doctor then?'

'Small matter of A-levels. Or rather, the lack of them.'

'Oh.'

He leant back in his chair and put his hands behind his head, his eyes on her face.

'You're looking at the last in a long line of dockers. My father, his father before him, etcetera etcetera.'

'Didn't you fancy it?'

'Didn't get the chance. They closed the docks on me. So I had to look elsewhere. I got a job as a hospital porter.'

'And worked your way up?'

'That's right.'

Katey smiled. 'You might be a doctor yet.'

He pulled a face. 'Too much like hard work.'

'And nursing isn't?'

'All that training and book work and exams every other week?' Larry shook his head disparagingly. 'No, I want to get where I'm going a lot quicker than that.'

'And where is it? Where you're going?'

'You said it.' He pointed towards the ceiling. 'Up.'

'Senior nursing officer?'

'*Principal* nursing officer at least.'

Katey gazed at him incredulously. 'Seriously?'

'Ambition's nothing to be ashamed of. It's good to have an aim in life, a goal . . .'

'Providing you're prepared to work for it,' Katey said pointedly.

'I am.'

'Ambition and nursing.' Katey cupped her chin in her hand and scrutinised him across the table. 'It's a funny combination isn't it?'

He smiled. 'Goes against the grain does it? Like male nurses?'

'What about the patients?' Katey asked, deliberately

140

dodging his question.

'What about them?'

'You haven't mentioned them at all, have you?'

He looked slightly irritated. 'Which automatically means I don't care about them I suppose?'

'Well, do you?'

He thought for a moment before answering. 'In my own way. I like to feel needed. Useful. I don't like to see unnecessary suffering. Like that fella in the ward, Whittaker. Working himself up when he could take a pill and sleep it off.'

'The easy solution,' Katey said. 'Take a pill and it'll go away.'

'What else can we do for them?'

'Talk to them,' Katey said simply. 'It's not as if he's in pain. He's worried. A tranquilliser won't cure that.'

'It'll dampen it a bit.'

'It protects *us,* that's all, so we don't have to put up with him worrying.'

Something in this simple statement seemed to aggravate Larry further. 'All right then, what are you waiting for?'

Katey frowned. 'How do you mean?'

'If you're so keen,' he said, 'why don't you go in there and talk him through it?'

Katey stared at him for a moment. 'Sounds like a challenge.'

'Maybe it is.'

'All right, I will.' She stood up and pushed the chair under the table. 'If he's still awake when I get there, that is ...'

'And if you don't get anywhere, I'll give him a tranquilliser.' Larry's tone exuded confidence, and Katey, now at the door, turned back to look at him.

'Suppose he's asleep?'

His lips curled into a lop-sided smile. 'Then we'll have both lost, won't we?'

Roy reached for the handle hanging from the frame above him, and shifted his body slightly, so that he could see Tom.

'Oi, Tom?'

Tom sighed, and rolled over. '*Now* what?'

'Which one do you fancy?'

Tom stared at him without replying.

'Of the nurses . . .' Roy grinned meaningfully, then added : 'Of course, if you prefer not to answer . . .'

'Neither of them.'

'No?'

'No,' Tom said flatly. 'Can I sleep now?'

'Be my guest.'

Tom rolled back and closed his eyes. Katey entered the ward and crossed to him. She was about to move away again, when he opened his eyes.

'I hope I didn't wake you.' Her voice was a whisper.

'It's all right. I can't sleep.'

'If it would help, I could . . .'

Tom cut her short. 'I've already said it a dozen times, I don't want any!' Katey stared at him in bewilderment. 'Sleeping pills,' Tom continued. 'I'd rather do without them.'

'I was only going to suggest that I made you a hot drink,' Katey said. 'You can have it in the kitchen if you like.'

He glanced at her, and then over at Roy, curiously watching them from his bed.

'All right. Thank you.'

The cocoa was dark and sweet. Tom sipped at it gingerly, watching Katey as she busied herself at the sink. She looked over at him and smiled.

'Expect you'll be relieved when the operation's over?'

He didn't answer. Katey dried her hands, and leant against the dresser. 'Imagine all the things you'll be able to do. Sport for example. Do you like sport?'

He gave a neutral little shrug by way of reply. Katey

pulled a wry face. This was going to be harder work than she thought. She looked down at his leg.

'Were you good at sport before . . . ?'

'I don't remember. I was only twelve when it happened.'

'Twelve?'

As if reading her mind, he said, 'I've left it a long time, I know.'

'You have.'

'I always seemed to find an excuse for not getting it done.'

Katey frowned. 'Did you need an excuse?'

He didn't reply straight away, instead he took a small sip of his cocoa. Finally he said in a low tone. 'It means a change in my life. I'm not very good at change . . . Not what you'd call adaptable.'

'Be a change for the better though surely? To get rid of that limp?'

He looked up at her, his blue eyes earnestly probing her face. He seemed to be weighing up whether or not to confide in her. 'What I said before . . .' he said at last . . . 'about not remembering if I was any good at sport. It wasn't true. I was never any good at it. Even as a kid.'

'That's nothing to be ashamed of.'

'That depends doesn't it?'

'On what?'

'The school you're at. Your parents' ambitions.' He paused. 'My father was football mad. Obsessed with it. He didn't play himself, he just loved to watch it. Dragged me to matches whenever he could. Made me sit up late watching them on television . . . Weekends he'd take me to the park. Other kids would be there, kicking a ball about. He wanted – ' he carefully corrected himself – 'expected me to join in.'

'And did you?'

'Not if I could help it.' The cocoa had left a brown ring

on his upper lip which he licked off. 'I used to make up excuses, even then, why I couldn't play. Pretend I was ill or . . .' He broke off, his voice hardening slightly. 'He didn't believe me though. My father. He was ashamed of me.' He glanced quickly at Katey, as if assessing the effect of his words. 'But after the accident, I had a real excuse, something he had to believe.'

'How did it happen, the accident?'

His face suddenly pulled into a frown. 'Why are you doing this?' He asked suspiciously. 'Talking to me like this?'

The question threw Katey for a moment, then she shrugged. 'Because I want to. I thought it might help.'

He stared at her for a moment. 'It's just that I'm not used to it. Talking about myself I mean.'

'You've done pretty well up until now.'

He looked down at his hands, resting on the table in front of him. The fingers were long and tapering, and he slowly drew them into his palms so his fists were like clenched balls. 'No one's been that interested before. Not genuinely interested. One can tell the difference.' He reached down and gently rubbed his bad leg. 'If anyone had asked me at the time, I'd have probably told them. But they didn't. They just made the assumption, and after a while I started to believe it too.'

'Believe what?'

He looked up at her. 'That it really was an accident.'

'What's the problem?' asked Larry.

Roy blinked at the torchlight shining into his eyes. 'I can't flaming sleep, mate. That's the flaming problem. Switch that thing off will you?'

Larry snapped off the torch and put on the reading light. He then picked up Roy's wrist and felt for his pulse. 'You had a sleeping pill did you?'

'For all the good it did.'

His pulse was slightly above normal. Larry lowered his arm, and pulled the blankets over him.

'You're written up for tranquillisers. Would you like one?'

'Will it help?'

'Might relax you.'

Roy shrugged indifferently. 'If you say so.'

Larry moved off to the drugs trolley and wheeled it to the foot of Roy's bed. He pulled the key ring from his pocket, unlocked the trolley, and picked up a small bottle of tranquillisers. Roy pushed himself up on his elbow to watch him.

'You ever take them?'

'What's that?'

'Them pills you're giving me.'

Larry grinned. 'Na.'

'Why's that?'

Larry shrugged. 'I'm not in hospital.'

'No?'

'I'm not *ill*.'

'Neither am I. A bit knocked about maybe, but not . . .'

'Here.' Larry passed Roy a small white pill, and watched while he swallowed it. Then he returned to the trolley. Roy sank back against his pillows, watching him.

'Funny, you being a nurse.'

Larry smiled. 'So people often say.'

'Like being a prison officer.'

Larry glanced at him. 'How d'you make that out?'

'We're all doing time together aren't we?' Roy looked down at the plaster encasing him. 'Me trapped in here. You trapped to your routine . . . Us both stuck in this dump.' He looked at Larry. 'Only difference is, you hold the keys, don't you?'

Larry looked down at the drugs keys in his hand, and slipped them into his pocket.

'Try and get some sleep, eh?' Quietly he pushed the trolley between the aisle of beds towards the desk, all the time aware of Roy's eyes, watching him from the other side of the ward.

'It's difficult.' Tom frowned slightly, searching for the right words. 'Difficult for you to understand I mean. As a man, certain things are expected of you. Certain accomplishments. And if you don't conform – ' he hesitated – 'You're ostracised. Labelled.' He seemed about to go on and then stopped.

'How did you do it?'

'I didn't do it intentionally,' Tom said hastily. 'I meant to put myself out of action, certainly, damage myself, but I didn't think further than that.' He broke off, and looked down at his leg, stretched out stiffly in front of him. 'I waited until they were all out. The family. My father had taken them to a football match. We had a row because I didn't want to go. He said things to me. Called me names. Vile names.' He flinched slightly at the memory. 'A father doesn't have the right to call his son names like that. No one has the right.' He paused and then went on. 'Outside my window there was this flat roof. Tarmaced you know? My mother used to keep plants on it. In pots. After they'd gone out, I . . . I went out on to the roof and . . .' He gave a small shrug . . . 'jumped.'

'Off a roof !' Katey exclaimed.

Tom nodded. 'When the time came to take the plaster off though . . . Well, I was dreading it. Because I knew it would all start up again. All the insinuations and . . . But they'd made a mess of it. The doctors. It hadn't set properly.' He looked back down at his leg. 'I was left with this. And they stopped. The rows. The insinuations. They all stopped ! It was so simple I wonder I didn't think of it before.'

'It can't have been that simple.'

He gave a small smile. 'It worked, didn't it?'

146

'What about all the things you missed out on?'

'Like what?'

'Like all the little things . . .' Katey searched for the right examples. 'Like dancing, and running and . . .'

'Everything has its penalty,' Tom replied simply. 'Its price. I don't regret it.' He hesitated, his face clouding. 'Perhaps, at the time, I'd think . . . maybe see someone of my own age . . . running . . . walking . . . moving. And I'd, just for a moment, regret it. Know that I'd closed that door for myself.' He glanced at Katey. 'It was around then they put me on sleeping pills. I was having trouble sleeping, so they put me on pills. Pretty soon I was on other pills. Tranquillisers. Anti-depressants. I'd have bottles of them by my bed.'

'But now you've stopped taking them?'

He nodded.

'And decided to have your leg done?'

'Yes.'

'Quite a new leaf.'

'It was getting out of hand. It got so I couldn't start the day without a pill. Couldn't do anything without one. So I weaned myself off them. One by one. To see how I'd cope as much as anything else.'

'And did you cope?'

He nodded again. 'Better than I thought.' He rubbed his leg. 'But there was still this, last but not least. So I thought, why not? And if I am the kind of person they accused me of – ' he reddened slightly – 'well, I'll just have to learn to cope with that too.'

A moment of silence followed, which Katey broke. 'Takes courage.'

'I've had seven years to work it up.' He drained the last of the cocoa and handed her the mug. 'Bit of luck, I might be able to sleep now.' He stood up, and gave her a small, embarrassed nod. 'Thanks for the drink.'

'Pleasure.'

'And the chat.'

Katey smiled. 'You did the talking, Tom.'

Slowly he smiled back. 'You did the listening.'

A moment later, Tom climbed into bed. He was just nestling into the pillows, when a familiar voice hissed at him from the next bed.

'Tom?'

Tom closed his eyes in despair. 'What now?'

'How'd you get on?'

'Eh?'

'With Nurse Betts. How'd you make out?'

'We talked,' Tom said simply.

'And?'

'And nothing.'

Roy frowned at himself in the dark. 'Just talked?'

'That's right.'

'Nothing else?'

'Nothing else.'

Roy hoisted himself up and looked over at Tom incredulously. 'What kind of bloke *are* you, anyway?'

Tom was suddenly engulfed by anger. He rolled over in the bed and faced Roy. 'I'll tell you what sort of bloke I am,' he said without bothering to lower his voice. 'I'm a bloke who's come in for an operation. Not to be goaded, or harassed, just to have an operation. Now, you have one of two choices. You can carry on as you are, in which case I'll ask to be transferred to another bed, or you can leave me in peace! In which case we might, possibly, be able to salvage something and make our stay here that much more pleasant. The choice is yours.' He turned away, resuming his former position so that his back was to Roy.

Had he still been facing his neighbour, and had the ward not been shrouded in darkness, he would have seen in the latter's face, not contempt, as he would have supposed, but something else : a grudging kind of respect.

At the desk at the other end of the ward, Larry frowned as he listened to the interchange. It wasn't Tom's words which puzzled him so much, as the sudden spirit that motivated them. Was it possible Katey *had* managed to get through to him? He tried to dismiss the thought, but it stubbornly persisted, and finally he succumbed to his curiosity, and quietly rose from the table, and tiptoed out of the ward.

Katey was at the kitchen sink, scouring the saucepan she had used for the cocoa. She looked up as Larry entered. 'Shouldn't one of us be on the ward?'

'You worry too much,' Larry said with an unperturbed shrug. 'Like him in there, born worriers.'

'You're the senior nurse. You'll be the one for the high jump if we're caught.'

'So why are you worried?'

'I was thinking of the patients,' Katey said pointedly. Larry said nothing. He sank his hands into his pockets and leaned against the wall, watching her. Unnerved by his silent scrutiny, Katey put down the saucepan, and started for the door.

'I'm sorry, but I really think one of us should be there.'

'You were happy enough to talk to him. Your Mr Whittaker.'

Katey paused and turned back. 'That was different.'

'Because you felt sorry for him?' There was definite sarcasm in his tone.

'If you like.'

'It's reserved for the patients is it? Your sympathy?'

Katey hesitated before replying. She suddenly felt apprehensive, as if all the events of the evening had been building to this one moment of confrontation.

"It's reserved for those who need it,' she said at last.

'And I don't?'

Katey smiled thinly. 'You seem to get by.'

'Appearances can be deceptive. Maybe I should bare my soul, tell you my innermost secrets. Would that do the trick?'

Katey gazed at him for a second before speaking. 'I really don't know what you're talking about.'

'I'm talking about you, love,' Larry said. 'The way through that starch armour of yours. Or is entry only permitted for the Whittakers of this world? The sick and infirm?'

'Meaning what?'

'Meaning you can cope with the patients, but anyone else, anyone fit and able-bodied, presents a threat. So away you run, tail between your legs.' He paused pointedly. 'Like now.'

'Nonsense!'

He smiled. 'How come you only reserve your chat for the patients then, and not for me?'

'I "reserve my chat for the patients" as you call it,' Katey said heatedly, 'because I'd rather talk to them than shovel them full of tranquillisers.'

'Which is what you reckon I do?'

'Well isn't it?'

'You'll do it too, love,' he said. 'When you've qualified. When you've got over the soothing-the-fevered-brow bit; the heart-to-heart-over-a-cup-of-cocoa bit. We all start off that way, you know. Even yours truly. Full of altruistic motives. It doesn't last though, take my word for it.' His tone was suddenly introspective. 'They drain it all out of you. Until you've no more advice to give, no more solace to extend. No more energy even to listen.'

'So you dish out tranquillisers instead?'

Larry roused himself and looked at her. He seemed suddenly angry. 'You think I enjoy it?'

'I think you enjoy the power of it, yes.'

'Power?' His brow creased into a frown.

'You're very quick to use those keys, aren't you?' Katey

said, nodding towards the drugs keys in his uniform pocket.

He gazed at her for a second. 'And *you're* very quick to jump to conclusions.' He pulled out the keys and held them out to her. 'If you think it's so easy, you take them for a bit.'

'Don't be daft.'

'Just for a minute, see how it feels.'

'You know I can't. I'm not qualified.'

'I'm not asking you to use them, love,' he said, taking a step towards her. 'Just hold them. See what it's like.'

Katey involuntarily took a step backwards. 'I told you, I'm not allowed to . . .'

Larry smiled, and pocketed the keys. 'They frighten you don't they? Shall I tell you why? For the same reason night duty frightens you, because these keys mean responsibility. You can open the trolley, and do as the doctor suggests. Or do it the hard way. Go it alone, and try and talk the patients through their problems. But that's risky, not just for you, but for them, because you might fail. So you end up ducking it. You end up using the keys and unlocking the magic box.'

'Because it's easier?'

'No, not because it's easier!' Larry said in exasperation. 'But because they're *there*. The keys are always there, don't you see? And with them the promise of pills, and instant relief. In the end you can't compete with them. What you have to offer is . . .' He broke off. 'Let's say you can't offer the same guaranteed results.'

'Who for?'

He frowned, bewildered. 'Eh?'

'Results for who?' Katey demanded. 'You or the patient?'

'I'm not with you, love . . .'

'You said, when we talked before, you said you wanted to go "up", remember?' Katey pointed a finger to the ceiling. 'And I'm just wondering who it is you really want the results for. I mean, a ward of nice quiet patients is bound to earn you a pat on the back isn't it?'

He gazed at her silently for a moment. 'You're quick all right,' he said at last. 'Quick to jump to conclusions, and quicker still to judge.'

'I told you,' Katey said, 'I'm just curious that's all.'

'About what, my motives?'

She shrugged. 'If you like.'

He looked at her thoughtfully. 'I see. Tell me something, if I was a woman, a female nurse, would you be equally suspicious?'

Katey frowned, his point was a good one, and she didn't have a ready answer for it. She was spared from replying by Myra Tripp, abruptly entering the kitchen.

'What's going on here?' Myra said, pulling up and looking at them both sharply. 'And why is the ward left unattended?'

Katey opened her mouth to reply, when Larry intervened. 'It's my fault, Miss Tripp . . .' he flashed a warning look at Katey . . . 'Nurse Betts wanted to return to the ward but I . . . Let's say we were having a difference of opinion, and I wanted to sort it out.'

Myra looked at him, and then turned to Katey. 'May I ask what this difference of opinion was all about?'

'As senior nurse on duty, Miss Tripp,' Larry said, 'don't you think it's *me* who should be answering the questions?'

Myra glanced back at him and frowned. 'Very well.' She nodded curtly to Katey. 'You may return to your duties.'

After a moment of hesitation, Katey left the room. Myra waited for the door to close behind her, before speaking.

'As senior nurse on duty,' she said, fixing her eyes on Larry, 'you should know better than to leave the ward unattended. May I also remind you that you have a duty not only to the patients, but to the students working under you . . .' She paused. 'I suppose I'd be totally wasting my time expecting *you* to tell me what this difference of opinion was about?'

Larry said nothing.

'Would I also be wasting my time to ask that it doesn't happen again?'

'No, Miss Tripp.'

'Consider it asked, then.' Myra moved to the door. 'And if anything like this re-occurs, I'll have no alternative but to report you. Do I make myself clear?'

'Yes, Miss Tripp.'

'You'd better see to your patients.'

There was a swish of starch and she was gone. Larry breathed a sigh of relief and started to make his way back to the ward. He was at the doors when Katey burst through them.

'Is she still here?'

'Eh?'

'Miss Tripp!' Katey said breathlessly. 'Is she still here?'

'What's the problem?'

'Roy Tucker . . .' Katey started to move into the corridor. 'I'd better fetch Miss Tripp.'

Larry caught her arm. 'Show me.'

'But . . .'

'*Show me.*' There was a sudden authority in his tone, and Katey responded to it. Swiftly she led the way back into the ward. Roy was clinging to the handle hanging from the frame above his bed, his face contorted with pain. As they approached him, he started to moan and cry out.

'O.K.' Larry said, quickly moving to his side. 'Where does it hurt?'

'My . . . aaaaaah!' A sudden spasm of pain prevented Roy from speaking.

'Is it your leg?'

Roy gasped, and nodded. Larry crossed to the end of the bed and threw back the blankets. The unplastered leg was stiffly stretched out on the sheets. As Katey watched, Larry started to massage the calf, with a hard, swirling motion.

153

'Now I want you to push against me, Roy,' he said. 'As hard as you can. When I give the word . . . PUSH!' Feebly Roy tried to push against Larry's grip.

'You can do better than that! Come on.'

Once again Roy pushed, this time with more effort.

'Atta boy! And once more for luck.'

Roy pushed again, then sank exhaustedly against the pillows. His thin face was covered in sweat.

'Better?' It was Katey who asked.

Weakly Roy nodded. Katey crossed to Larry, who was still massaging the leg. He glanced at her anxious face.

'Cheer up. Haven't you ever seen cramp before?'

She nodded wanly. 'It wasn't that I was thinking of. I was thinking how I was all for calling Miss Tripp.'

Larry grinned. 'Just as well you didn't. We're not exactly in her hit parade as it is.' He turned to Roy. 'Just breathe in and out a few times. Try and relax, OK?'

Roy blinked at him blearily. 'I couldn't have one of them pills could I? To help us?'

Larry was just reaching into his pocket for the drug keys, when he felt Katey's eyes upon him. He glanced at her, deliberated a moment, withdrew his hand, and addressed himself to Roy.

'Why not try by yourself this time? You can't expect them to do all the work.' He looked up and met Katey's eyes. Slowly they smiled at each other. As they moved away from the bed, Tom rolled over to look at Roy. He reminded him of a broken puppet, surrounded by the wires of his traction frame, and the sight suddenly aroused an acute compassion in Tom. 'Are you all right?'

Roy turned to look at him, his face still moist with sweat. 'You what?'

'I asked,' Tom said, already regretting it, 'if you were all right?'

'In the flaming pink.' Roy turned dispiritedly away and

154

Tom did the same. Why *do* you bother, he asked himself. He shut his eyes wearily. He'd made his gesture towards friendship, if Roy was too stubborn to accept it, that was his problem.

'Tom?'

Tom opened his eyes.

'Eh, Tom?'

'What now?'

'Goodnight, mate.' Roy paused. 'What's left of it.'

'Cramp, and I was about to send an S.O.S.' Katey said ruefully. They were back at the desk, surrounded by the sleeping patients.

'It's easy to think the worst about these things,' Larry replied. 'Particularly at night. Things always seem much worse at night.'

Katey glanced at him. 'What I said earlier . . .' She began hesitantly. 'About being suspicious of your . . .'

Larry cut her short. 'We both said a lot of things,' he said gently. 'It's like I said, it's easy to think the worst at night.' He smiled his lop-sided grin. 'Why don't you go over to the canteen. Get us something to eat?'

'I was going to make a start on the pressure sores.'

'I can do that.'

Katey seemed about to rise, then paused. 'No, you go. I'd rather stay here.'

He shot her a shrewd look. 'Means you'll be on the ward alone for a bit . . . ?'

She gave a tiny shrug. 'I'll have to manage won't I? It's time I did.'

He continued looking at her a moment, then stood up.

'It's all yours then.' He started to move away, then turned back, grinning. 'You must look me up, when I'm Principal Nursing Officer.' He winked slyly. 'I'll see you're all right.'

Katey smiled, and watched as he quietly made his way out of the ward. Then she glanced over to the window. It had stopped raining.

In the same series :

Angels　　Paula Milne and Leslie Duxbury

The stories of six young student nurses – their first impressions of hospital life and how they cope with everyday problems.

Flights of Angels　　Paula Milne

Follows the careers of student Pat into her second year, Jo who passes her finals, Maureen who gains experience as a District Nurse, and Shirley, now exalted to the status of Staff Nurse.

(both books published jointly with Pan Books Ltd)